THE CRI

PHOEBE ATWOOD TAYLOR

THE
CRIMINAL
C.O.D.

An Asey Mayo Cape Cod Mystery

A Foul Play Press Book

THE COUNTRYMAN PRESS
Woodstock, Vermont

THE CRIMINAL C.O.D.

ONE

~~~~~~

"MOTHER, *where* is my car?" Jane Lennox pointed an accusing forefinger at the blank walls of the unlighted garage. "Mother, where *is* my car? Mother, where— Oh, damn, that's too dramatic!"

She got up from the running board of the black sedan, ground out her cigarette on the cement floor, and tried the sentence again. A standing speech was always more effective.

"Mother, where is *my* car?"

It was such a simple sentence, she thought. Five simple, forthright words. But the more she practised, the harder it was to get the proper intonation, the exact blending of curiosity, annoyance, and injured innocence.

She was severely hampered, furthermore, by knowing perfectly well just where her car was, and who had it, and why. That knowledge was burning her up, from the toe of her spike heeled pumps to the topmost brown curl on her head.

"*Mother,* where is my car? Mother, where is my *car.* Mother— Well, here goes!"

Jane braced herself as she heard her mother's footsteps outside on the gravel path, and drew two full breaths from the diaphragm.

Then, as Mrs. Lennox snapped on the garage lights, Jane spoke her piece.

"Mother, where is my car?"

Kate Lennox gave a startled little cry.

"Why, Jane dear! What are you doing out here in the dark? I thought you were having dinner with Ty and his father!"

"Mother," Jane said sternly, "where is my car?"

"Why, darling, you told me you were having dinner with the Brickers, and not to expect you back till after the dedication was over— Are you going to the first show at the movies? I'll be glad to drop you off."

"That," Jane said, "is certainly white of you! But don't evade the issue. Where's my car?"

"I keep telling you, dear, I thought you'd be busy all evening, so—"

"So," Jane forgot her determination to keep cool at all costs, "so you went and lent my roadster again to the People's Choice! Didn't you?"

"Jane dear, I do wish you wouldn't speak so flippantly about Henry. Henry Slocum is a nice boy, and he can't go to the dedication in that old rattle-trap of his. With the Governor and everyone there, it simply wouldn't be fitting!"

"If you ask me," Jane told her hotly, "Henry P. Slocum's rattletrap fits him like a glove. And it's a hell of a lot more fitting and democratic than my chromium plated Porter Twelve!"

"Dear," Kate Lennox looked hurt, "if you're planning to go somewhere, you can always take the beachwagon."

"Darling," Jane retorted, "if you can stop thinking about Henry Slocum and that damn school dedication long enough to remember the day of the week, you'll find it's Thursday. William and Mary took the beachwagon this noon. Remember?"

"Oh, so they did. Well, I can drop you off anywhere. Of course, it would please Henry enormously if you changed your mind and came along to the school. Why don't you come with me?"

"I wouldn't go to that damned school dedication if it were the last place on earth! I've heard Henry P. Slocum rehearse his damned speech so many damned times, I gag at the thought of it—"

"Really, you mustn't damn things so," her mother interrupted. "I know you don't mean anything by it, but other people don't understand. It reflects on your father and me."

"Mother," Jane said with dignity, "will you bear in mind that I'm no longer a babe in arms? Will you try to remember that I'm twenty-one, practically twenty-two?"

Before she realized that she had laid herself wide open, her mother thrust home with the ease born of long experience.

"I'm sure, dear, you don't act it, do you? Now, I simply must get along. It's nearly seven."

"It's just exactly six-ten," Jane said, "and the Quashnet Community School doesn't begin its official opening fish fry and war dance till eight. You've got plenty of time to settle—"

"But you know Henry expects me at seven. You heard him say so. I must go, dear."

Kate Lennox started toward the sedan, but Jane continued to stand directly in her way.

"Mother, if your young rail splitter beats Uncle Jeff and gets elected to the legislature, d'you expect to sit at his elbow and put words into his mouth, and jiggle his arm when his grammar starts skidding? D'you realize what you're letting yourself in for?"

"I've no fault to find with your uncle," Kate Lennox said. "Jeff Gage has always tried to repre-

THE CRIMINAL C.O.D. 11

sent this district as well as he could. But Jeff's being one of the family doesn't close my eyes to the fact that Quashnet Township and Cape Cod need new political blood. So I'm helping Henry. I feel it's a civic duty. I must get along!"

Jane put out her hand.

"Wait. This is important. You mean, you intend to string along with Henry Slocum to the bitter end, in spite of all this gossip there is about you already? Mother, you must have heard some of this filthy gossip!"

Kate Lennox sighed. "Dear, I haven't the time to waste listening to gossip. Nor would you, if you only had something bigger and more worthwhile to think about than golf and sailing. I told your father last week that we simply must find something to take up your mind— Oh, Nosey, you mustn't! Bad doggie! Down! Down, Nosey!"

She tried to shove away the brown spaniel who had bounded into the garage and started to jump madly about her.

"Jane, take Nosey back to the house, will you, dear? Before he gets me all muddy."

"Is that *all* you have to say?" Jane demanded.

"Quickly, dear. I can't get muddy. I've got to sit up on the platform. Do grab him! Thanks, dear. Yes, I think we'd better make plans for you to open a nice shop this winter. Yarns, or knitting, or refugee handiwork, or something like that. Your sister loved her little shop. Are you quite sure you won't come with me?"

"Is that," Jane was breathing hard, "your last word on the topic of Henry P. Slocum?"

"I'm trying very hard, dear, not to point out that you're being silly, and just a little theatrical. Coming?"

"No!" Jane stamped her foot. "No, I'm not! And when Horseface Henry gets through using my car, please see it's washed and swept out. Last time you presented it to him, I spent half a day cleaning out the beer cans and beer stains. *And* the hairpins. And if you feel you have to drag him and his pals back here for a snack, for my sake, see they don't throw their live cigar butts on the game room floor! They've ruined all the numbers on the shuffle board."

"If the Governor should care to drop over—"

"The hell," Jane said, "with the Governor! And the hell with Henry P. Slocum, the People's Choice!"

"Really, dear!"

"Yes, really! And don't be surprised, Mother darling, if you and your precious Henry begin to run into little problems! Don't say that you weren't warned, Mother darling!"

Jane stalked out of the garage and up the path to the house, with Nosey bounding along beside her.

Kate Lennox looked thoughtfully after her youngest daughter.

Of her three children, Jane had given her the least trouble. While Emmet punched policemen and Anise practically eloped with riding masters, Jane stayed dutifully in the schools selected for her, calmly conforming to all their rules and regulations. While Emmet was being returned from his annual midyear runaway trip to sea, while Anise was being brought back from her passionate pursuit of one orchestra leader or another, it was always comforting to know that Jane was safely playing hockey and eating prunes and getting math prizes, never causing anyone a moment's anxiety. Now that Emmet and Anise were married and out of the way, Kate Lennox had looked forward to a comparatively tranquil existence. Up to the last three months, everything had been fine.

But since June, when Ty Bricker came to Quashnet, Jane had not been her sweet, conforming self. Even her vocabulary was different. And she said the most puzzling things.

As soon as elections were over, Mrs. Lennox decided, she would devote herself to the problem of what to do about Jane and Ty. Not that she had anything against Ty Bricker, except that he had no purpose in life. No useful, worthwhile occupation. If only Henry Slocum, she thought wistfully, could have had half of Ty's chances, and even a tenth of the Bricker money!

Mrs. Lennox remembered belatedly that she herself had a purpose. Henry was probably walking back and forth outside the new school this minute, waiting for her to hear his speech once more. This school dedication was going to prove a heaven-sent opportunity for the dear boy to show himself to the Governor and the rest of the county bigwigs. And Henry's speech really justified all the days she'd spent on it. It was earnest, sincere, not too polished, and nicely spiced with local dry humor. In short, she decided as she backed out the sedan, it was a gem of a speech, a speech which would in all probability launch Henry on a long, successful political career.

Before she came to the main road at the end of Cod Point Lane, Mrs. Lennox had dreamed Henry Slocum into the senate, with Slocum for President clubs springing up like mushrooms all over the country. She would be there too, of course, discreetly in the background, probably wearing grey. Perhaps, in the course of time, she might even get to be an ambassadress to one of the Scandinavian countries.

But in the Lennox house on Cod Point, Jane was proceeding with more realistic plans for the future of Henry P. Slocum.

After a brisk telephone conversation with Ty Bricker, Jane marched along the hall to the south wing. The study door was closed, but she pounded at it, and kept on pounding until it was opened.

Her father stood there, his pipe in one hand, his eyeshade pushed up over his forehead, and his old plaid dressing gown hanging loosely over his tall, thin figure.

"Busy, Dad?"

"Yes," Charles Lennox said. "Very. I shall resent being disturbed even for just a moment."

"But I want to speak to you—"

"Your allowance check is on your mother's desk."

"Oh, money! I don't want money! Don't you think I ever think of anything but money?"

"Money," Charles Lennox said, "is a very useful commodity, and nothing to be blasé about."

He cleared his throat and put his pipe back in his mouth.

"Dad, you're not so busy you can't talk!"

"I am. I've just found a delightful item in those records Mark sent over, and I wish to investigate it tonight, and discuss it with Mark before he leaves tomorrow. It casts a totally new light on Ethan Pilcher's decision to have Quashnet separate from Pochet."

"Can't you think of anything but your old history of Quashnet?"

"Jane," Charles said, "I'm sure other things beckon to you. Don't you feel like making fudge? You make excellent fudge. Go make me a plate of fudge, there's a good child."

Jane thrust her foot into the crack of the door.

"Dad, I've *got* to talk with you! It's something really vital, and I want your—"

"Want to open that shop your mother mentioned, eh? Well, tell me tomorrow."

"No!" Jane felt like screaming. "I don't want to open any shop, ever! I want—"

"New car?"

"I have a car!" Jane said. "Except when Henry Slocum has it!"

"Slocum? Oh, that new garage fellow. Tell him I said he did a terrible job on the beachwagon."

"He's not the new garage man! Father, don't you even know who Henry Slocum *is?*"

"Frankly, I'm not interested."

"Oh, you're not! Well, would it interest you to know that the whole Cape is buzzing with gossip about him and Mother? Would it interest you to know that his name is constantly linked with hers?"

Charles smiled.

"My dear, any number of people have had their names linked with your mother's."

"And you don't care?"

"Well, I never cared for the man who taught her the conga, but then I never do care for perfumed men." Charles looked at her quizzically. "Aren't you seething more than usual?"

"Seething? Father, I'm so seething mad, I can hardly talk! Listen, don't you care for any of us, for any of the family?"

"I'm devoted to you. But right now I'm busy with the history of Quashnet."

"You know we exist?"

"I'm pointedly aware of you, dear."

"Father!" Jane grabbed the door handle and pushed against it. "Dad! You've got to listen! Mother's making a fool of herself with that foul Slocum!"

"Your mother never makes a fool of herself," Charles said. "You can't make a fool of a woman with all her self-confidence."

"Father, do you love her?"

"What an absurd question, Jane! Good night."

"You have *got* to listen to me! Mother's going around with Henry Slocum, do you hear me? She pretends it's just her civic duty to help him in his campaign against Uncle Jeff, but the whole Cape is talking, and gossiping, and calling her nasty names, and laughing at you! Don't you see? It isn't all idle chatter! It's serious, nasty gossip!"

"I've long since ceased to listen to Cape gossip," Charles told her. "I'd close my ears to it if I were you, too. It's always nasty and invariably untrue. If your mother dabbles in politics, she'll find it all highly instructive. She's never dabbled in politics before, has she? Well, she'll doubtless learn many interesting things. She always does."

"But don't you care that—"

"When your mother is gripped by one of her curiosity spells," Charles said patiently, "she investigates. At the moment, she's investigating politics. When she's learned enough, I dare say she'll find something else to investigate. She always does."

"You can stand there," Jane said, "and tell me that you don't care if your wife, my mother, is getting herself and you and the family made a laughing-stock! That—"

"Jane," Charles said, "I think if you considered this in a less heated mood, you'd find you've been turning molehills into a mountain range. You're letting unfounded personal prejudices sway you to inaccurate conclusions and extremely silly exaggerations. You must learn to be more objective."

So many words came to Jane's tongue that she couldn't sort them out into a coherent sentence.

"I had the same trouble with your sister," Charles went on, "till she opened her dress shop, and learned the virtues of patience and humility and charity. I'm now going to work on the history of Quashnet, and if you're unwise enough to bang at my door or annoy me in any way, I shall throw the ink at you. Good night."

Jane surveyed the door that closed with finality in front of her.

"All right!" she said bitterly. "Go write the history of Quashnet, but don't be surprised if a lot of new data come tumbling into your life! Don't say that I didn't warn you, either! Don't—"

She ducked as the door opened suddenly, and an ink bottle thudded against the wall behind her.

"I am a man of my word," Charles Lennox said, and shut the study door.

Jane watched the ink trickle down the white wainscoting and seep into the best hooked flower rug. Then, restraining her impulse to mop the mess up, she marched back along the hall.

She had done her best to appeal to everyone's reason and better judgment, and all people did was to treat her like a child, and hurl ink bottles at her!

Now, she thought as she stamped up two flights of stairs to the attic, she was going to take matters into her own hands. It was high time people realized that she didn't go in for idle threats. When she warned people, she meant business.

With a vicious tug, Jane yanked at the dangling string that snapped on the cluster of electric lights in the cupola above her. Before this night was over, the Lennox family was going to understand that she was a girl of her word, too!

Fifteen minutes later, dressed in slacks and sneakers and a polo coat, Jane banged the front door behind her, and set out to take her part in the drama of forever erasing from the Lennox household the blot that was Henry P. Slocum. If she had any sort of luck, she thought with satisfaction, she would also manage to put a pretty effective crimp in his political career.

It was darker outside than Jane had anticipated, and she thought with regret of her flashlight, now reposing in the glove compartment of her roadster. There were probably other flashlights in the house, but only William and Mary ever knew which ones worked, and Jane preferred boiling herself in oil to going back and asking her father for his. It was colder than she expected, too. More like November than September. There was a whiff of fog in the breeze blowing in from the bay, and a chilly, damp smell from the mists curling in the meadows beyond.

Jane buttoned up her coat. She hadn't intended to take Nosey along, but she was glad when the dog came bounding up. There was no telling how long a wait she had before her, and Nosey would help while away the time.

She walked past the family boat house, along the shore path to the old sail loft. It seemed to grow darker, the farther she got from the house, and Jane paused for a moment and turned to see if the cupola lights were burning. Even if their pleasant glow didn't keep her out of the poison ivy and blackberry vines, at least they were serving another useful purpose.

Nosey's sudden outburst of excited barking made her pause again, and consider the skunk problem. After a cautious advance on the object of his attentions, Jane was relieved to find that it was only a stone.

"Here, stupid!" She picked it up and threw it. "Run! Go get it!"

But Nosey only barked, and bounded off in the opposite direction.

That was characteristic of the animal, Jane thought. In fact, she decided as she turned back to the path, Nosey was a characteristic dog for the Lennox family to own. Nobody else would ever

tolerate or cherish such a stupid, stringy, nonde-
script little thing. Her mother had saved him from
a horrid death during her anti-vivisectionist days,
and as a reward, Nosey had ruined every rug in the
Boston house, chewed up all the draperies, and
deliberately guided burglars to the hidden wall safe
in the library. The burglars said so in court. And
still her mother called Nosey a dear, darling doggie, and her father referred to him with pride as a
rugged individualist!

Jane's irritation mounted as she stepped into a
puddle left by the afternoon tide, and felt the
clammy cold oozing through her sneakers. Apparently this was one of those days when nothing
was to be spared her, not even wet feet. Probably
before long the mist would change to a hard, driving rain, and Nosey would round up a few skunks.

The long, barnlike outlines of the old sail loft
finally loomed ahead.

Jane stopped, listened, and peered ineffectually
through the darkness. Then, according to plan, she
sat down on the boundary stone and composed
herself for a good long wait.

The lights of the town twinkled dimly across the
black expanse of Quashnet Bay, and the blur of
automobile headlights converging toward the new
school indicated that the Bay Road was already in
the throes of a traffic jam. With a sniff, Jane recalled

that widening and resurfacing the Bay Road was one of Henry P. Slocum's more fervent campaign promises. And how mad her mother got when she and Ty pointed out that it was a purely selfish gesture on his part. Henry used the road more than anyone else, since his house was at one end, and his store at the other.

Ty Bricker was the only person who had reacted logically to this Slocum mess, Jane thought. Ty understood. And the way he'd figured everything out tonight was pretty masterly.

Nosey pattered up after a while and tenderly dropped a dead horseshoe crab at her feet. Before she could reprove him, he pattered over to the sail loft, and scratched persistently at the side door until he managed to get it open.

Presently sounds ensued which indicated that he was engaging in his favorite pastime of catching rats. The loft was disgustingly full of rats this summer. Mrs. Lennox had been too busy with Slocum's campaign to give her usual parties there, and the yearly extermination had slipped her mind entirely.

A sinister silence following a series of short yelps caused Jane to stand up and march over to the loft door.

"Nosey," she said crossly, "come here! Don't you *dare* eat that rat! Remember what happened the last time! Drop it!''

Nosey's answering snort was a derisive challenge.

"All right, disgusting!" Jane said. "Then I'll come take it away from you. Hear me? I'll shake it out of you!"

In the far corner, Nosey capered with pleasure at the prospect of a friendly tug.

"All right, I'm coming!" Jane said. "And you'll regret making me stumble around this pitch black rat hole after you, my little canine pal!"

Kicking the door wide open, Jane stepped over the high threshold and started after Nosey.

At once she tripped and fell headlong.

Her first confused thought was that she must somehow have stumbled over the dog.

Then, as she got to her knees and groped, Jane let out a scream which sent Nosey flying past her from the corner like a frightened flash of lightning.

It was an arm which had tripped her.

An outstretched arm, limply lying on the loft floor. A limp, tweed covered arm attached to a limp, crumpled figure.

While one part of her brain was absorbing the significance of that kind of limpness, Jane remembered that Henry Slocum had spent the morning displaying his new tweed overcoat to her mother.

TWO

~~~~~~

JANE'S second scream was such a thing of unadulterated horror that the sound of it demoralized her completely.

Her flight from the sail loft was even more headlong and precipitate than Nosey's.

Outside the door, Jane lost her balance, lurched, and toppled over a mound of oyster shells that cut her hands and bruised her face, but she was hardly conscious of either the shells or the damage. Picking herself up, she ran forward blindly.

And with every stride, her terror grew.

Now something was following her, coming closer and closer to her heels. Now it was almost catching up.

With a sob, Jane forced her feet to fly faster.

It was no relief when she found out that the pursuing thing was only Nosey. His low, snarling growl and his paws scrunching along the shell-covered road ruts only added to Jane's panic. They were the touch of reality, the tangible proof that all this horribleness actually existed in fact.

Neither the girl nor the dog paid any attention to the direction they were taking. Neither was aware they were heading directly toward the main road. Neither saw the headlights of the car approaching at such tremendous speed, or even felt the tarred road under their weary feet. They just kept on, blindly dashing forward.

Then, for a hideous split second, the girl and the dog and the car seemed to meet.

Jane had no breath to scream again, no strength to move another step. She stood there as if she had suddenly taken root, watching blankly while the car heaved itself up on its rear tires like something in a nightmare.

Years seemed to pass while the car wavered above her shoulder, almost within her grasp. Then it swerved and settled on its side with the rasping sound of crumpling metal.

Standing like a statue, Jane listened to the noise.

She had a queer feeling that this was all part of an animated cartoon she was viewing on a screen, one of those three dimensional films you looked at through red and green celluloid glasses. Because if it had been a real car coming at her that fast, it couldn't have stopped like that without killing her.

No car could have stopped like that. Cars couldn't rear on their hind legs like a squirrel!

She was beginning to be able to breathe again without her ears hurting, but the pain that had been in her throat was now unaccountably located in her right hand.

Looking down, Jane found that she had instinctively grabbed Nosey's collar, and now she was gripping it so hard that the metal name plate was cutting into her palm.

She let go.

Nosey shook himself, pattered over to the car, and circled tentatively around it.

Jane moistened her lips. Once again Nosey was providing the touch of reality. That was the way he always circled around cars, as though they might turn out to be something that would lean over and take a bite out of him.

Suddenly a tall man in a yachting cap appeared around the front of the car. His slow deliberate steps as he strolled toward her made Jane think of her father about to administer a spanking when she was a child.

Jane swallowed.

"Did you lose control?" she asked.

It was not what she meant to say, at all. She intended to ask if he were hurt, and to explain that in her excitement, she hadn't seen the car coming, and she was sorry for the accident, and that it was all her fault. But she was still incapable of coordinating her thoughts and her feelings with what were apparently more tangible facts.

The man pushed his yachting cap back on his head, and rather pointedly thrust his hands into his coat pockets.

"Not," he said, "yet."

"What?" His answer bewildered Jane.

"You asked if I'd lost control," the man said, "an' I told you. I said, not yet. But if I was you, I don't think I'd try me."

Jane could tell by that slow drawl that the man was a Cape Codder. And his appearance was vaguely familiar. She ought to know who he was.

"Tomorrow I wouldn't of minded," the man went on. "But tonight, I——"

"Why, it's a Sixteen!" Jane took her first good look at the car lying on its side, and realized that it was a chromium finished roadster like her own, only this was even longer and more bullet-like. "It's a Porter Sixteen! Then you must be——"

"Right now," the man said bitterly, "you could hardly call that a Porter one an' a half. Listen, I don't dare let myself go, but I got to get this much off my chest, young woman! The next time you feel like combinin' fifty yard dashes with readin' the letterin' on my radiator, you please do it when I'm parked, an' not while I'm in motion!"

"I didn't even know you were coming!" Jane said. "I didn't see you. Look, you must—"

"You didn't see me coming?" the man interrupted. "You didn't, huh? Didn't see me coming! Will you turn your head to the left? Thanks. What you see before you is a level, lighted highway, stretchin' straight as a string to Quashnet. Now turn right. There's another stretch of straight road goin' like an arrow into Pochet village. You mean to stand there an' tell me you couldn't see my car comin'?"

"I mean," Jane returned, "I didn't see your car! I wasn't looking for cars! I wasn't thinking about cars! I didn't care two cents about cars! And—"

"An' you don't care two cents for the mess you've made of mine. You don't regret it a bit, do you?"

Jane did regret it, but her regret was beginning to be overshadowed by resentment. This man didn't have to rub it in!

"I suppose," she said, "you think I jumped in front of your car on purpose?"

"Wa-el," the man drawled, "you got to admit it

looked that way from where I was sittin'. I'll even go so far's to say that you couldn't've jumped more plumb square in front of me if you'd practised the timin' for the greater part of your life."

"Is that so! Well, I certainly expected that the great Asey Mayo— You *are* Asey Mayo, aren't you? I thought so." Jane pointed toward the roadster. "I recognized your car."

"No, you never recognized that car," Asey Mayo told her with what was for him an unusual amount of rancor. "Not that car. That's a brand new custom model built to my own specifications, an' I had it just half an hour before you leapt onto my horizon. That's why I said I wished you'd waited till tomorrow, after I'd had a chance to try her out. That's why I'm feelin'—"

"Sore!" Jane said violently.

"Nope. I'm feelin' a deep an' gnawin' disappointment."

"So am I!" Jane said. "You're one of the biggest disappointments I ever suffered, Mr. Asey Mayo! Why, Uncle Jeff's bragged about you for years. His friend, the great detective. The brainy Homespun Sleuth! The dry, humorous Codfish Sherlock! The great, unruffled Mayo, who smells out trouble with a clothespin over his nose! The great racing driver, the great mechanic, the great—"

"I think," Asey said, "that'll be just about enough of that from you, youngster!"

Jane ignored his quiet warning.

"Why, to hear Uncle talk, you'd think you were a combination of Sherlock Holmes and Will Rogers and Abraham Lincoln and God! But as far as I can see, you're a dumb sorehead Cape Codder, beefing because your pretty car's got a scratch!"

"Youngster," Asey said, "one more crack, and I'll take my hands out of my pockets, and I'll spank you within an inch of your life!"

"I'm sick and tired," Jane suddenly began to sob, "of being treated like a child! You've nearly killed me, and there's that dead corpse, and—and—my feet are wet!"

The tears rolled down Jane's cheeks, and dripped off the point of her chin. She made a valiant effort to stop and pull herself together, but the more she dabbed at her eyes, the faster the tears gushed out.

Asey stared at her, and then walked rapidly over to his car. He fished around inside, and returned with a small flashlight.

He raised his eyebrows at the picture which the beam revealed.

The girl's face was bruised, her forehead was smeared with dirt. There were smears of what seemed to be blood caked on her hands, and red stains on the front of her light coat. Her eyes were puffed and bloodshot.

"Youngster," Asey said, "what's been goin' on? Who are you?"

"I'm Jane Lennox. From Cod Point."

"Oh." The sympathetic note went out of Asey's voice. "Oh, Jane Lennox, huh?"

"What d'you mean, 'Oh, Jane Lennox, huh?' in that tone of voice?"

"Are you by any chance," Asey inquired, "the Jane Lennox who teamed up with Ty Bricker an' called the Coast Guard to say there was a German submarine layin' mines in Quashnet Bay?"

Jane gulped. She would have been less surprised if the man had pulled out a gun and shot her.

"You are, aren't you?" Asey persisted.

"What of it?" Jane said. "We only wondered if people could cope with that sort of thing, if it did happen. It was just a—a test case. How did you ever find out?"

"The gov'ment," Asey said, "was so touched by the seemin' interest in national preparedness an' defense, they sent a G-man down to look into things an' find out why. He never got to you kids, because he happened to land on a couple of bona fide spies pryin' around the radio station in Chatham. You just missed a nice jam session."

"I don't believe it! And I think you're the horridest man!"

"I'm sure you do. An' you're the same Jane Lennox that come with young Bricker when he hoaxed the Weesit Sewin' Circle, lecturin' on his fake trek through Darkest Africa. You sung native songs in blackface—"

He broke off suddenly and waved the little flashlight at an approaching car.

Jane heard only snatches of the conversation between Asey and the driver, something about sending Sam's wrecker, and some heavy humor concerning the fate of fast drivers. How, she thought in honest bewilderment, had that man ever found out! No one had ever tumbled to that Sewing Circle business!

"In blackface," Asey continued as the car drove on, "an' in dialect. You're *that* Jane Lennox?"

"How did you find out those things?"

"Just," Asey said, "a little homespun sleuthin'. Now, Miss Jane Lennox, you run along!"

"But look here!" Jane said. "I just found a corpse!"

"Uh-huh."

"But I did!"

"Yup. Now, beat it."

"It's lying there now, on the floor of our sail loft!"

"You go right back," Asey said gently, "an' tell it to get up."

"You think I'm joking?"

"Miss Lennox," Asey said, "if anyone else come to me an' said there was a body in your sail loft, I'd believe 'em. But I heard only this afternoon that you an' Master Bricker had some plans brewin' about takin' someone to town—"

"I don't believe you!" Jane said. "Who told you so?"

"It come over the grapevine." Asey enjoyed the expression on the girl's face.

"What grapevine?"

"The twenty-two party line, over home in Well-fleet. My Cousin Jennie overheard one of the Bricker servants talkin' to a friend," Asey explained, "an' she mentioned it to me, in the course of conversation. But I never thought I was the one you was plannin' to have fun with. How'd you figure it out?"

Jane didn't answer. She couldn't.

"I s'pose," Asey said, "you heard my new car was bein' delivered, an' you guessed I'd be tryin' it out on this stretch, seein' it's the only straightaway in miles. Huh. Well, Miss Lennox, you took a terrible chance, jumpin' at me. I don't know why the car stopped in time, even with them new brakes. But no matter what you two sprouts think, even a fake corpse isn't funny. You take my word for it, an' run along."

"Now you look here! You—"

"I know. I'm a horrid thing to spoil your act, but you hop along an' tell young Bricker to get up from the floor. Then both of you phone Sam's garage to hurry up with the wrecker."

"You come to the sail loft!" Jane said. "You—"

Asey grabbed her arm and pulled her toward him as a car sped past and then ground to a stop half a mile beyond. The car backed up, and the driver asked solicitously who had been killed.

"Nobody, thanks," Asey said. "But I would like to have Sam Paine's wrecker. Ask somebody in Pochet to put in a call an' hurry him up, will you?"

"Asey Mayo," Jane said furiously as the car sped away, "I don't think you'd smell trouble if someone rubbed it with garlic and limburger! You listen to me, you—you Codfish Sherlock, you! I went to our sail loft—"

"Cheever's old sail loft on the bay shore, near your place?"

"Yes. And the dog—"

"What dog?"

"Didn't you see the dog with me? He's here—Well, he *was* here. Anyway, Nosey went into the loft, d'you hear me? And he caught a rat. I heard him. And I went barging inside to keep him from eating it, because rats make him sick as a horse. And I tripped over it!"

"The rat?"

"This isn't any time for vaudeville!" Jane said. "I tripped over this arm. This body. That's why I was running, you idiot! That's why I didn't see your car coming! I was so scared to death, I wouldn't have seen ten thousand cars! I didn't even know I was running this way. I was just running. And I'm really sorry about the new roadster, and father'll pay for a new one. And now, you come along and see this body, and stop being so coy!"

Asey hesitated.

The girl did sound sincere. But she had sounded sincere when she roused out the Coast Guard and the Navy. She had sounded sincere at the Sewing Circle, when she sang her African war chants. Asey himself had heard her from the back room, when he delivered a cake that his Cousin Jennie had forgotten to take with her. And although you had to discount about ninety-nine percent of what came over Jennie's twenty-two telephone line, you could usually find a grain of truth buried deep in the gossip.

"What did you go to the sail loft for?" Asey asked suddenly.

"Why," Jane said, "why—er—why, I just walked down that way. I was taking a walk. Exercising the dog. I didn't have any ulterior motives. I just happened purely by the remotest chance to stroll in that direction."

It occurred to her in a flash that she and Ty Bricker were in for it if Asey Mayo found out that they'd really had a plan afoot.

The thought stunned her. The possible complications that might arise were so ghastly that she thrust them out of her mind at once. Nothing so horrible could ever happen. It simply couldn't.

Besides, the more immediate problem of Ty himself was claiming her attention. Sooner or later he would come bursting in on the scene, probably dripping with details. Somehow, Jane thought grimly, Ty would have to be warned and shut up. Luckily, the boy was quick to take a cue.

"Just chance." Jane wet her lips. "Just the purest chance."

"I see," Asey said. "Fate led your footsteps to the sail loft. Was it a man or a woman?"

"You didn't think I was making all this to-do over the corpse of a baby chick, did you? It was a man, of course—" Jane stopped. "Well, at least I *think* it was a man."

"Did you look?"

Jane shuddered. "I did not! I ran!"

"Who was it, anyone you know?"

"Did you," Jane returned, "ever fall over a corpse?"

"Wa-el, no," Asey said. "I can't say as I ever did. But if I found one, I think I'd be curious to know who it was."

Jane was thinking very quickly.

"But there is no light in the sail loft, you know."

"Wasn't your own flash workin'?"

"I didn't have one. I keep mine in the car, like you do. Mr. Mayo, let's get this all straightened out." Jane's voice was the earnest, genuine, straight-from-the-shoulder voice that had always so impressed teachers and convinced them of her sterling worth. "What you know of me is unfortunate. I mean, it's unfortunate you should have found out about the Coast Guard and the Sewing Circle. But didn't you ever do crazy things when you were a boy? Even my father used to put cows in belfries, but he's considered a very solid citizen now."

"Meanin'," Asey said, "that I ain't come in contact with your better nature?"

Jane couldn't tell whether he was being serious or not.

"Well, yes. I mean, I read to the blind, and run around rolling bandages for the Red Cross, and I used to be given Bibles for good conduct in school. And really, I'm not being funny about this corpse! I'm telling you the truth! Look. Look at my hands. D'you see these cuts and scratches? I fell down on the oyster shells when I ran away from the sail loft. Can't you see I'm not lying?"

"What was this plan that you an' Bricker had up your sleeves?" Asey wanted to know.

Jane drew a long breath. There wasn't going to be any use pretending that she and Ty were innocent of any plans. Not with this man. But she ought to be able to skirt the truth and get away with it. She'd have to.

"Well," she said, "I'll come clean on that, too. I went to the loft to meet Ty. You see, the new school's being dedicated tonight, and Mother's being very civic and sitting on the platform with the Governor and Uncle Jeff, and we— Well, we were planning to play a joke on her. We wanted to keep away from the house, because Father's there, and we didn't want him to find out." It was easy to improvise as you went along, Jane discovered. Easier than she'd expected. She continued with more confidence. "You see, Father's busy writing the history of Quashnet, and he's not much in the mood for practical jokes. And now, will you *please* come to the loft? Now that I think of it, you're just exactly the person I'd have called if I'd been capable of any constructive thinking."

Asey grinned. "That's very flatterin' of you."

"I mean it. I— Well, I feel pretty sorry about everything, Mr. Mayo. I— Well, I'm sorry."

"Wa-el," Asey said, "since you've up an' admitted it, I might's well admit I'm sort of sorry, too. I *was* almighty sore at you, an' sore about my car, an' I oughtn't to have lit into you like that. An' I ought to have known you wasn't fakin'. I'm sorry. Let's get along."

They walked across the tarred road and set off briskly down the shell-rutted lane.

"Didn't notice anythin' suspicious, did you?" Asey inquired. "No funny noises, nobody around, nothin' out of the ordinary?"

"Not a thing," Jane said. "It was chilly, and damp, and dark, but everything seemed all right."

"No cars?"

Jane shook her head. "No. And I'd have noticed any cars, too, because this is the only road leading to the loft from the main road. In fact, it's the only way to get there by car. We use it. We drive all the way down Point Lane from the house, and then turn and go all the way back to the loft on this. It's like going the length of a hairpin to cross the ends, but Father got tired of having cars stuck in the swamp by the shore."

"I thought there was another lane," Asey said. "Below this."

"Oh, you mean the old road. Yes. But Father had that barred long ago. The parkers got to be a nuisance. Mr. Mayo, this—this corpse is a grim business!"

Asey nodded.

"You don't seem to be taking it— Well, what I mean is, you don't seem very grim," Jane said. "You seem sort of optimistic!"

"I'm hopin'," Asey told her, "that your corpse'll turn out to be somethin' like a coil of rope, or a bundle of cloths—"

"What?"

"That's happened before, you know. Things at night can be sort of terrifyin', an' that loft's a gloomy old place. An' your description's just vague enough—"

"Look here, I know a limp arm when I feel it!" Jane said. "And the arm was attached to a limp body! And if I fall headlong over an arm, and it doesn't move, and nobody says anything, I think you can come to the conclusion that the arm and the body aren't alive!"

"Yup," Asey said, "but—"

"There's such a thing," Jane said, "as carrying skepticism and doubt too far! I assure you, I can tell a limp arm from a coil of rope practically any day or night of the week! There—there's the pile of shells I fell over, ahead. See?"

Asey focused his flashlight on them.

"Uh-huh."

"And there's the side door! I'll stay here," Jane said, "and you can go in and see for yourself! And if you don't find a corpse in there, you—well, you can give me that spanking you threatened me with!"

Jane sat down and waited a little breathlessly while Asey continued on to the side door.

She had a pretty good idea of what was going to happen next. Asey Mayo would recognize Slocum, of course. He couldn't help it, with all those campaign poster pictures tacked around on phone poles.

And when Asey came out, he'd say, "That is the body of Henry Slocum!" And then, Jane decided, she'd give a good scream and pretend to faint. That was the best idea, because then she wouldn't have to answer any questions, and Asey would have to carry her up to the house. Then she'd have a chance to get hold of Ty by phone and warn him. Because heaven only knew where Ty was, and if he'd only started to carry out just the smallest fraction of their plan, Ty would be in trouble. He might even need to provide himself with an alibi.

Asey was coming out.

"Well?" Jane stood up.

"Think quick, youngster!" Asey said sternly. "If you can think of anything good enough, say it quick! If you can't, I'll count ten an' give you a head start! But if I lay hands on you, you're goin' to get the tannin' you been askin' for!"

Jane snatched the flashlight from his hand and darted into the loft.

The place was empty.

There was no body there.

But as she stood in the doorway, frantically sweeping the floor with the flash, Jane heard a dragging, slapping sound of something moving in the tool room beyond.

"Asey!" Jane howled. "Asey! Come— Oh. It's only *you*, is it?"

Nosey, who had poked his head around the door into the beam of light, hurriedly withdrew.

A second later he reappeared and trotted over toward Jane.

"Asey!" Jane screamed. "Asey! Asey, see what he's got! See what he's *got!*"

THREE

BEFORE Asey could step past Jane into the loft, Nosey slipped past him and was bounding out into the night.

"Asey, did you see what that beast had in his mouth? It was a scalp!"

"It was a rat," Asey said.

"You didn't see it! You couldn't have. He went by you too fast. I tell you, it was a scalp! It was hair!"

"Blonde, I s'pose?" Asey inquired drily.

Jane ignored his irony. "No, it looked more reddish. Go after that dog and get it, quick!"

"Have you an' Comrade Bricker set up strings somewheres so I can take a nice header?"

"Stop being like this! Stop it!" Jane said wildly. "There *was* a body, right by this door. Right here!" She pointed. "And the arm was here. When I stepped over the threshold in the dark, I tripped right over it. If you hadn't stalled around being so coy and suspicious out on the road, you'd have got here and found it before someone took it away! You're going to look awfully silly when people hear you let Henry Slocum's body be spirited away right under your nose!"

Asey stared at her.

"Whose body?"

"Henry Slocum's! No, I *didn't* see his face! But I'm sure it was Henry Slocum. He had on a tweed coat. His new tweed coat! No, go find Nosey. If you can't do anything about the body, at least you ought to be able to hang on to the only clew there is!"

Jane turned and went out the door and started calling.

"Here, Nosey, Nosey! Oh, if that dog had an ounce of sense, this wouldn't have happened! Asey, can't you come out and find that dog? He's probably burying that hair in a skunk hole. Here, Nosey, Nosey! Good heavens, he's actually minding for a change! Asey, come here, he's still got it! Look!"

She focused the light on Nosey as he pattered up.

"It's a wig!" Asey said. "A red wig. Huh. Come here, feller, an' give it to me!"

Nosey waited till Asey was a foot away, and then

he capered off through the bushes, with the red wig still in his mouth.

"Oh, he thinks it's a game of tag!" Jane said in despair. "And I suppose if we chase him, he'll just keep it up indefinitely. He can. And if we don't chase him, he'll go and bury it somewhere. What'll we do?"

"You stay here an' make enticin' sounds," Asey said, "an' see if you can't lure him into bringin' it to you. Look, Miss Lennox, I'm pretty puzzled. What makes you think this body could possibly have been Henry Slocum? You say you didn't see any more'n a limp arm, an'— Well, with the whole wide world to pick from, what makes you think it was *his* arm? Why are you so decided about that?"

"The tweed. He was going to wear his new tweed coat to the school dedication tonight. You see," Jane explained hurriedly, "the family's been interested in his campaign, and he's been around the house a lot, and this morning he showed us his new tweed coat. He was very proud of it."

"But you say you just touched the arm," Asey said. "How in the world could you tell it was Slocum, just from that?"

"Well, it's a little difficult to explain," Jane said. "Henry thought it was the most magnificent garment he ever saw in his life, but— Well, his experience with tweed's a little limited. I mean, it wasn't tweed like that jacket you're wearing. Or Dad's coats. Or Ty's. It was rough and hairy and bulky. I just touched that arm for a second, but I recognized the stuff. D'you understand the kind I mean? You send your measurements by mail, and the coat comes the next day."

Asey nodded. "I know. Padded shoulders, an' a belt you tie, an' dogs bark at you. Yup. Offhand, I'd say there was about two hundred in Wellfleet. I see. Now you stay here an' entice your dog, while I go inside for a moment. Give me the light, will you?"

"Why?" Jane asked.

Asey pointed out that he couldn't see in the dark. "An' I want to take a brief look around before we do some checkin' up—"

"Why the red wig, you mean? Why should anyone leave a red wig here, and how'd the body disappear? No cars went up the lane! Where'd it go? How'd it get away?"

Asey shrugged expressively, and went inside the loft.

For his part, he was still more concerned with the problem of whether there had been a body in the first place.

Not that he any longer doubted the girl's sincerity. He was quite sure that she had started down to the sail loft to meet young Bricker, and that she had stumbled over what she thought was an arm in a tweed sleeve. After all, Asey thought, a detail like mail order house tweed had a ring of authenticity. A girl like Jane Lennox couldn't make up something like mail order tweed on the spur of the moment. Very likely the girl was right about the arm. But it still didn't seem possible that the arm was a part of the corpse of Henry Slocum.

Asey flashed the light around the loft. The place was one large rectangle inside, about forty feet long and twenty wide. It had been nearly three times as long, he remembered, in the days when it was a real sail loft, but in the course of the years, the back part had been cut down.

He walked slowly along near the wall, past a rough, fieldstone fireplace, and any quantity of rough, weathered chairs and benches. There was an old upright piano, too, and a dozen pungent lobster pots, apparently piled up for the winter. He opened the door of the closet-like tool room that jutted out of the corner. It was empty except for a rusty kerosene stove and an assortment of cast-off dishes.

There were more chairs and benches along the opposite wall, an old-fashioned victrola with a bulging horn, and a horsehair sofa whose springs protruded above the seat in fungus-like hummocks of cotton wool stuffing.

The place was far from being in apple pie order, but on the other hand, there was no indication that any violent struggles had taken place. Nothing was tipped or overturned. There were no puddles of blood on the old oak planked floor, no knives, or guns, or other lethal weapons.

"Huh," Asey said.

He clambered up a ladder to the open storage garret that ran along the front of the building. Nothing had been disturbed up there. The dust of decades lay undisturbed over a miscellaneous collection of old lumber and old furniture.

Asey climbed down.

Yes, very likely the girl had fallen over an outstretched arm in a tweed sleeve, but he was still far from convinced that a corpse was involved.

He paused for a moment, and noticed suddenly that there was a door in the front of the loft, under the garret. It was clearly an afterthought door, cut in after someone had rather haphazardly rebuilt the wall.

Asey walked over to the door, thrust it open, and looked out. In the old days a wharf had extended out before the building, but now there was only a verandah-like segment of perhaps ten feet, stopped by a flimsy railing. With his flash, he picked out half a dozen of the old pilings sticking out of the water.

He stepped outside and considered the situation. If this tweedy arm had belonged to a body, this front door and wharf might well be the solution of how the body had disappeared. The body could simply have been put into a boat after the girl left. That would explain the absence of any car along the lane.

But as he thought it over, Asey decided that the boat solution was not very sensible. A body that disappeared involved at least one other person. That meant that at least two people had come by boat to the loft, where, presumably, one had allowed himself to be made a corpse without putting up any sort of struggle whatsoever. If one person had come by boat to meet another person at the loft, then the latter would in all likelihood have left a car in the lane. In the first place, it would be a little foolish to put in at the loft to kill someone. In the second place, the loft seemed an odd meeting place. With all the miles of dunes and woods on Cape Cod, a loft on someone else's property didn't seem the ideal spot to leave corpses.

It was all too complicated, Asey decided. The

tweedy arm doubtless belonged to a sleeping tramp, who had probably taken to his heels as soon as the girl rushed away.

As he leaned forward and looked at the waves lapping around the piles, he heard something creak behind him.

Jane tiptoed to his side.

"Asey, keep on flashing the light. Listen, I think there's someone watching us!"

"What? Where?"

"Over in the pine grove. I've heard Nosey run over there and yip four different times. I wouldn't think anything about his just going and yipping, but the last two times there's been a funny noise as if someone was trying to drive him off. I—I'm afraid."

"Wouldn't be your friend, Ty Bricker, would it?"

"Oh, no! Ty would come in a car, and you'd hear him. He's an overt person. Besides, Nosey would make a tremendous fuss over Ty. They adore each other. Asey, what'll we do?"

Asey thought for a moment.

"You take the light an' stay here. I'll do a little circlin' around an' see what's goin' on."

"But suppose you find someone?"

"It'd be a pleasure," Asey told her. "I'd enjoy

findin' something I could put my finger on."

Before Jane realized his intentions, Asey swung off the verandah onto one of the old pilings at the side. She heard a thud as he jumped from it to the shore.

Jane blinked. Her brother Emmet was supposed to have been a crack broad jumper, but he'd never been able to make that particular jump without getting soaked, although he'd tried for years. It began to look as if there might be something in this Mayo the Great propaganda after all.

She only wished she could convince him that there had been a body. If only she could find some clew, something tangible, some sort of proof.

Jane went back into the loft and set out with some determination to see if she couldn't bring to light at least a shred of tweed.

The room had a cold, evil feeling about it that made shivers run up and down Jane's spine. If she could only explain that feeling in words to Asey, he'd never entertain any more doubts about that arm!

She knelt down and searched the floor near the side door inch by inch with the flashlight. There had to be a clew. And she had to find it.

She admitted to herself simultaneously that she wished she couldn't. Because finding proof of that body might very possibly turn out to be worse than not finding proof. Things were going to be pretty grim if she found something that convinced Asey, and then it came out in the wash that Ty had gone through with all those plans.

Jane sighed, and shivered. But she kept on doggedly hunting.

In the meantime, Asey made his way quietly along the far side of the loft outside.

At the corner, he stopped and listened.

The dog, Nosey, appeared out of the shadows, sniffed him, and trotted off in the direction of the pines.

A few seconds later, Asey heard him yipping, and then he heard the unmistakable sound of something small and hard falling in the underbrush. Someone was throwing stones in an effort to distract the dog.

At last, Asey thought, here was something going on that was caused by a person who was there!

Noiselessly, he proceeded along through the beach grass and the bushes at the left of the lane. Then he crossed it and started to circle back to the pines.

Ten minutes elapsed before he spotted the figure of a man standing beside one of the trees, and the chances were that he would have missed him entirely if it hadn't been for the dog returning for another investigation.

Asey advanced by inches, and thanked heaven that Nosey seemed willing to accept him as a part of the landscape.

The man wore a dark suit and also a dark hat, a fact which impressed Asey at once. Native Cape Codders were not inclined to wear hats. They went in for caps. And even when dressed in their best, practically no Cape Codder he knew would venture into the woods at night wearing a brimmed felt hat. Offhand, Asey couldn't even think of a single summer visitor of his acquaintance who even owned a hat.

Asey reached out his hand.

Another step, and he'd have the fellow by the scruff of his neck.

His hand was almost touching the man's coat collar when Jane screamed.

It was the third time she had screamed that night, and she was improving with practice.

And the sound sent the dark suited man running as though he had been shot from a gun.

Asey leapt after him.

The man turned his head for a startled second, and then lengthened his stride.

At the same time, the dog appeared, and decided without any hesitation that Asey was the person he preferred to run with. But after a hundred yards, Nosey abruptly changed his mind. His quick, right angle swerve sent Asey into a headlong sprawl.

By the time Asey had picked himself up, the footsteps of the dark suited man sounded yards to his left, far beyond the loft and the shell road, headed for the highway.

Limping a little, Asey started after him, and almost immediately found himself involved with a swamp. He was still hunting a way around it when he heard the sound of a motor starting.

The fellow had a car on the old lane, the lane Jane assured him was barred!

With an exclamation of annoyance, Asey listened to the rising whine of the motor as the car was whipped into gear, and then he turned around and started back to the sail loft.

He was sure of one thing. Of all the nights in his life, this was the craziest and the slaphappiest. He never remembered experiencing anything even remotely similar to it.

He thought of how it would sound if you summed it up for someone.

"Yes, a girl found a body, but it was whisked

away. A dog found a red wig, and he whisked that away. I found a strange man, and he whisked himself away."

Just summing it up yourself sounded pretty bizarre, Asey thought.

He shook his head. He felt thwarted.

But he was sure of one other thing. He was going to get to the bottom of things. Every single last thing, including the body, the red wig, and the man with the hat.

And also what the girl had been screaming about.

He found Jane in the process of climbing down from the peaked roof of the sail loft by way of the drain pipe at the rear.

"He went *that* way!" she told him breathlessly. "Oh, damn, I've got another splinter. That way, Asey. He drove smack around the bars, and turned toward Pochet on the main road."

"So?" Asey said, and sat down on the ground.

"Don't you hear? He went *that* way!"

"I heard. It's a nice thing to know. I'll always think of that feller," Asey said, "as bein' the man who went that way."

"Aren't you going after him?"

"With what?"

"Well, we can go up to the house and phone the

Pochet four corners cop, and have the car headed off, can't we?"

"We could," Asey said, "if we knew who he was."

"Don't you know? Didn't you see him?"

"I saw a chunk of his chin for about one-hundredth of a second. You know, I wish you—"

"For the love of heaven, what were you doing all that time? What was he doing? Did he have the body with him? Didn't you find out anything?"

"Miss Lennox," Asey said, "I wish you'd do somethin' about your timing. If you'd timed things better, you wouldn't have made me ruin my car. If you'd held onto that screech of yours just a wee mite longer, I'd have had that feller. I was a hair's breadth from grabbin' him when you let loose. You'd have thought it was a startin' gun, the way he lit off."

"Oh, dear!" Jane said. "I can't get out of the wrong, can I? I'm sorry. Didn't you get any idea of what this man looked like?"

"He wore a dark felt hat with a turn-down brim," Asey said. "Know anyone that wears a hat? Does Slocum?"

"Slocum wears caps exclusively," Jane said. "He unearthed a derby for the school dedication, but Mother— I mean, Mother and Father finally talked him out of it. There's something sinister about someone in a hat, isn't there? Even Father doesn't wear one down here. Asey, wouldn't it do any good to phone Pochet and have all cars stopped? Can't you do that on the chance of finding the car with the body?''

Asey shook his head. " 'Fraid not. You're assumin' he's goin' to drive smack through the Pochet four corners, an' for all you know, he may have just gone up the road a piece, an' then doubled back when he felt sure he wasn't bein' followed.''

Jane sighed. "I never thought of that. Asey, have you got any of this figured out?''

"Not much," Asey said honestly. "Have you?''

"Well, I've been trying. Of course, it's easier for me, because I'm sure there was a body. I think that man must have been hiding here in the loft when I came in after Nosey and tripped. And I think that after I dashed out, he picked up the body and ran for his car that was parked in the old lane. Does that seem logical?''

"Uh-huh. It seems simpler," Asey said, "than the boat theory I was playin' with.''

"I tried boats," Jane said, "but it was too hard. I kept having a man left over, or a boat left over. Look, Asey, I think this man put the body in the car, and then he came back for the wig. And then he heard us coming, and was waiting there to see what we were up to. And I'm almost wondering if maybe Nosey didn't have that wig, and not a rat, in the first place. I can't find any trace on the floor of his having toyed with a rat. Anyway, I think he came back for the wig. And the flask."

"The what?"

"The flask. I found it. That's why I screamed," Jane said. "I was trying to find a clew to prove I was telling you the truth, and I found the flask. Here."

Asey took the small, leather covered pocket flask from her and examined it under the flashlight.

"It's Henry Slocum's," Jane said. "See the initials, E. L.?"

Asey grinned. "The H and S of Henry Slocum bein' silent like the *p* in pneumonia, huh?"

"It was my brother Emmet's flask. One of those cunning things that one of his girls gave him for Christmas. But it holds only a gill, and it weighed a ton, and Emmet never used it. But Henry Slocum saw it a couple of weeks ago, and pined for it, and Mother gave— Mother and Father gave it to him, in a generous moment. It was back under the legs of one of the benches, as if it had rolled against 'em, and stuck there. Now, isn't that proof?"

She was so proud of her discovery, Asey decided

not to point out that while the flask might be the property of Henry Slocum, finding it now in the loft didn't necessarily mean that it had just been left there.

"Tell you what," he said, "let's go to the house an' do some phonin', an' investigate things at source."

"What do you mean?"

"Wa-el, s'pose we phone the new school," Asey said, "an' see whether or not Henry Slocum is there as you say he planned to be."

"And if he isn't?"

"Let's save that particular bridge," Asey said. "Come on. What's the shortest way to the house?"

"The path, but don't let's take it," Jane said. "The tide's terribly high, and we'll either have to slosh through it or cut around the swamp, and I haven't the spirit to do either, now. Let's go back the shell lane, and cut over to the Point Lane. It's much easier going. By the way, have you caught sight of Nosey lately?"

"Not since he tripped me— Did I tell you about that? I'd still have caught that feller if Nosey hadn't done a double-shuffle about-face right under my feet."

Jane giggled. "I know just what you mean. He did the same thing to William at dinner, night before last. William was bringing in the raspberry sauce. Dad says it's Nosey's dramatic sense."

"He seems to pick dramatic moments," Asey said. "Want me to whistle for him?"

They both whistled, without the slightest response from Nosey.

"He's probably back in the house," Jane said, "sitting snugly in front of Dad's fire. Dad keeps a wooden walk outside his window and when Nosey wants to come in, he trots up and scratches on the window pane. Let's get along. I'm beginning to feel my age. I'm dead."

They had progressed most of the length of the Point Lane when the motorcycle cop rode past them, and then stopped.

He greeted Asey genially.

"Hi! Well, if they got you going on this Slocum hunt, I guess the guy's dead all right!"

FOUR

JANE'S fingers dug into Asey's arm, and she barely restrained another scream.

"Found any trace of him?" the cop continued.

"Not a trace," Asey said. "Er—what's the consensus, Jake?"

"Huh?"

"What do people think?"

"About Slocum? Oh, they made an announcement at the school that he'd been unavoidably detained on account of a sudden illness," Jake said. "They seemed to swallow that all right."

"But what do you think?" Asey asked.

"Me? Well, at first I thought the guy'd probably got cold feet. Seems he was going to make his first big speech, in front of the Governor and everybody, and so when they said he hadn't turned up, I just thought the guy was scared. I been to places before when guys that had to speak didn't turn up. Then that woman started raising hell."

"Which woman?"

"This Mrs. Lennox. She lives here, up at the house on the point. I guess she's a pretty good pal of this Slocum—"

"Mr. Slocum," Jane interrupted, "is a friend of our family, officer. We've known him for many years. What did Mother think happened to him?"

Jake swallowed.

"Well, to tell you the truth, she's been pretty excited, she has. She kept saying that nothing would stop Slocum from giving that speech unless it was foul play. She almost got into a fight with Jeff Gage. I thought she was going to paste him one, one time."

"With Uncle Jeff!" It was Jane's turn to swallow. "Oh!"

"Yeah. She said it was his fault Slocum hadn't turned up. But he calmed her down, and said he'd find Slocum for her. That all happened out in the hall, and I heard 'em. So Gage asked us to get Slocum, so the three of us, me and Green and Brogna, we left Kelly to look after the Governor, and we set out. But hell, we can't find him!"

"Been to his house?"

"Yeah. He lives the hell and gone out at the end of the Bay Road. We been there. But he ain't there. We hunted all around the place, too. His own car's there, but it seems he was using another, a Porter Twelve that belonged to Mrs. Lennox—"

"Mine," Jane said. "I lent it to him."

"Oh. Well, it wasn't there, and he wasn't there, so it looks like he left in it. But we can't find that Porter anywhere. We been over every road around town, and called up Pochet, and Wellfleet, and all around, but nobody's seen it, even. We thought we had him when we found a wreck out on the highway that Sam Paine was taking away. But it was your Sixteen, Sam said."

"That's right," Asey said. "Did Sam think it was in bad shape?"

"He didn't say anything except if I seen you, to have you call him, and he'd send your old car anywhere you wanted. It didn't look too bad, Asey. Just crumpled some. I seen lots worse."

"That helps," Asey said. "Huh. So you can't find any sign of Slocum?"

The cop shook his head.

"No. Some of his friends are out, but they're stuck, too. I just come up here because Mrs. Lennox asked me to, the last time I went back to school."

"Poor Mum!" Jane said. "I bet she's simply a frazzle!"

"She's pretty excited, but I tell you, when she slips back to her seat on the platform, you'd never think she had nothing worrying her mind."

Jane nodded. She knew that bland look of her

mother's. It often fooled people into thinking that she was at peace with the world, just as her casually matter of fact manner sometimes made people think she was a fool. Jane had seen more than one store keeper blink when Kate Lennox added a column of figures backwards before he'd reached the second item.

"Well," the cop said, "if you haven't seen Slocum around here, I won't bother to go any farther. I'll get along back to the school. Guess there's been some dirty work, hey, Asey?"

He obviously wanted to be able to report Asey's opinions, so Asey played safe.

"Wa-el, I don't know. Lots of things can happen to people without there bein' any actual fatalities, Jake. You say you've phoned around?"

"Phoned? Say, one of the pay stations in the school basement's out of order, it's so full of coins! We've phoned, we've combed, we scoured, we done everything!"

"Been over all the back roads? He might be hung up on a lane, somewheres."

"I been over more rut roads tonight," Jake said, "than when I used to chase rum runners. I been on rut roads you wouldn't believe unless you rode over 'em on one of these things. I even been out to the back shore. And the way I feel now, I don't care if they never find Slocum! Kelly's going to take my place, now, and I'll stand around and decorate the school for a while!"

"Well?" Jane said after the cop roared away. "Well?"

"The noise you hear in my throat," Asey told her, "is words being eaten. Youngster, this begins to look bad. Are you sure that the plans you made for the joke you was goin' to play on your mother didn't maybe involve Slocum's disappearin'?"

"They shouldn't," Jane said. "I can't think of any reason why he shouldn't turn up at the school."

It was comforting, Jane thought to herself, to know that was the truth.

"Where's your pal, Ty?"

"I'm going to phone and find out."

"There's no remote chance," Asey said, "that Ty an' Slocum might be together?"

"Ty and Henry," Jane said, "aren't very chummy. They're not deadly enemies, or anything like that. But I think it's safe to say you wouldn't ever find them together. Not in a social way."

They walked along in silence to the house.

As they passed the study window, Jane tugged at Asey's elbow.

"Will you look in there!"

Inside, Charles Lennox was scrambling around the rug on all fours, playing with Nosey.

"See what he's got on his head?" Jane pointed. "D'you see what he's wearing?"

Charles Lennox was wearing the red wig.

Still holding Asey's arm, Jane marched to the front door, and along to her father's study.

"Father," she said, "for heaven's sake, where did you get that wig!"

"Nosey brought it in." Charles got to his feet and looked interestedly at Asey. "Good evening. I don't think we've ever met, but of course I recognize you from pictures. Did you get my message?"

Asey looked puzzled. "Message?"

"I see that you haven't. I telephoned you tonight, and left a message with your housekeeper— Poor dear, she seemed terribly distraught. She said you were trying out a new car, and I got the impression she expected you to return on a stretcher. I wanted to know, Mr. Mayo, if you happened to have any of the Ethan Pilcher records. I know he was an ancestor of yours—"

"Dad!" Jane said. "This isn't any time to delve into the history of Quashnet! Where did you get that wig?"

"I told you, dear, Nosey just presented me with

it. You can't imagine," Charles took the wig off and surveyed it, "what a wig does to you. It's tonic, like a paper hat."

"Yes, I noticed you're letting yourself go!" Jane said. "And after all your stern talk about working far into the night, too!"

"Your mother put a stop to that," Charles said. "She's kept calling up and calling up, wanting Henry. And Jane, I simply can *not* find Henry. I've hunted this house from attic to cellar, and I can *not* find that fur."

"That *what?*"

"Fur. Doesn't she call that fox fur piece 'Henry'?"

"That's Henri*etta!* Aunt Henrietta gave it to her, and it looked like her, so Emmet named it Henrietta! Dad, she didn't mean that! She meant—"

"I didn't think she *could* mean that," Charles said, "but that's what she kept asking for, Jane. I don't think I ever heard your mother ask for anything so many times, and so strongly! Why, she even said something about my calling her at the school if I found Henry, and she'd send a car to fetch him!"

"Dad, Mother meant Henry Slocum!"

"Who?" Charles asked.

"Henry Slocum!" Jane said. "Slocum, the—"

"Oh, I remember. The garage man. Isn't it lucky," Charles said, "that I didn't find that fur piece! Your mother would have been pretty annoyed if I'd sent a fur piece to her by car, when she wanted a garage man. But Jane, she never said there was anything wrong with the sedan! Why would she want the garage man? And why on earth would she expect me to have the garage man here? That's silly!"

Jane's exclamation of mingled irritation and despair caused Asey to turn and look at her rather carefully as she stood by the study lamp. It was really the first good opportunity he'd had to see what she looked like, and he found that she was more attractive than he'd suspected. In spite of her disheveled brown curls and the smudges of dirt on her forehead, her face was arresting because of its swift changes of expression. When Jane Lennox felt things, she showed that she felt them. And right now, her brown eyes were sparkling with indignation at her father.

Suddenly Asey remembered the details concerning the Lennox family which had been eluding him all evening. It was more grapevine gossip from Jennie's twenty-two line, and it involved the outrageous behavior of Mrs. Lennox in spending so much of her time and money on young Henry

Slocum and his campaign. He remembered Jennie and her friend, Carrie Higgins, clucking their tongues over Mrs. Lennox's outrageous behavior.

And he also remembered how Jane had pointedly referred to Slocum as a friend of her family's, a friend of her mother and father, and how she had picked up the cop and squelched him when he started to comment on Mrs. Lennox and Slocum.

"Slocum, Father!" Jane said. "Slocum! The one who's trying to beat Uncle Jeff for the legislature! *That* Henry Slocum! *Must* you be so absent-minded?"

"Oh, the tall one with the dark hair and that space between his front teeth! Oh, of course," Charles said. "The one that's been underfoot so much. To be sure! But you know, I never have been able to think of him as Henry Slocum. I always think of him as Erasmus Larrabee."

"Who?" Jane said. "What?"

"Erasmus Larrabee. He used to sit next to me in college chapel," Charles explained. "Larrabee, Lennox, Logan, Luke. That was the way we went for four years. Anyway, Erasmus Larrabee was tall and dark, and he had a space between his front teeth like that, too. Amazing fellow. Got to be a lama, or a llama— Which do I mean, one 'l' or two?"

Asey chuckled.

"That sort of depends on whether he got to be a beast or a priest, don't it?"

"Well, he was a little of both," Charles said. "Fantastic fellow— Jane, while I think of it, you and I must conspire to keep this Slocum fellow from rehearsing speeches in the herb garden. He trampled the chives again this morning."

Asey sat down on the arm of a chair. He was beginning to enjoy Mr. Lennox thoroughly. But Jane continued to look despairing.

"Father— Oh, dear! You think he's funny, too, don't you, Asey! But if you had to live with this sort of thing, you'd understand how there are times when you are compelled to call out the Coast Guard. If you didn't have some outlet, like calling out the Coast Guard, then—"

"Jane," Charles interrupted, "does the Coast Guard have anything to do with all this business of your mother's having lost that fellow who looks like Larrabee?"

"No. I was only—"

"Well, then, don't let's waste time rambling on about the Coast Guard!" Charles became suddenly efficient. "Let's help your mother out, and find this Henry Hokum for her."

Jane reminded him that the name was Slocum.

"Can't you remember it, Father? Can't you even *try?*" she added.

"I'm trying, but it's very difficult when I've always thought of him under a different name. Now I don't think he's in the house. I went over and into everything very thoroughly while I was hunting that infernal fox fur. I'm sure I'd have seen the fellow if he'd happened to be around. Mayo, this sort of thing is in your line. Where do you think we might find Henry Slocum?"

"I'm beginnin'," Asey said, "to wish I knew, myself. Say, can I see that red wig a second, please?"

"Certainly! Nosey brought it in to me with great pride, just a few minutes before you came. You know," Charles said, "there's apparently no end to the things that dog can unearth. Once he came home dragging half of a grass skirt, and a headband with African designs. Swahili, I think. Remember that episode, Jane?"

Jane's cheeks were very pink. "Yes. But where's the red wig? I thought you put that on the floor, didn't you? Over by your desk."

The red wig was nowhere to be found.

Neither was Nosey.

"Is there any way the dog can get out by himself?" Asey asked. "No? Then if he's still indoors, maybe we could take a look around an' find where he's hid the wig."

Both Jane and her father smiled at the thought.

"It's Nosey's custom," Charles explained, "to wait till you've hunted in one spot, and then he hides what you're after in that very place. Er—unless you feel *very* deeply about the wig, suppose we leave it for the moment, and set out. I do feel that we ought to try and find Henry Slocum for Kate. Suppose you get out the beachwagon, Jane. That has big tires, and we can go practically anywhere in it—"

"William and Mary have the beachwagon," Jane said. "Mother has the sedan. Slocum has my car. And—"

"D'you think it's quite wise of you to lend people that car?" Charles asked. "Didn't we find some clause in the insurance policy about the responsibility of the owner when a car is loaned?"

Jane bit her lip. To be blamed for Henry Slocum's having her car was almost the last straw. But she couldn't go into that matter now, with Asey there.

"Mother and I," she said, "decided that Henry'd better have the roadster tonight, to go to the school dedication in style. His car's not very reliable.

And," she drew a long breath, "and I might as well tell you that I wrecked Asey's new Porter Sixteen tonight. I walked in front of him, and he smashed up in order to avoid killing me and Nosey. It was all my fault."

"So that's why you both look so unsettled!" Charles looked unsettled, too, as he sat down. "Mayo, I'm sorry. Will you get a new car and send the bill to me? I'm only glad that you weren't hurt. No," he waved aside Asey's protests. "Please don't let's discuss the matter. I assure you that my daughter and my dog are worth a roadster, and I don't want to think of what might have happened if someone else had been at the wheel. Tell me, how can we go about finding Henry Slocum?"

"I'll have Sam bring my old car here," Asey said. "Where's the phone, Jane?"

After he finished with Sam, he called Jane back to the hall.

"Will you telephone your friend, Ty?" he asked. "I'd like to know what's become of him."

"So," Jane said, "would I!"

She gave the Brickers' number, and waited. Then she gave the number again. Then she spoke to the supervisor.

"I can't understand this," she said at last to

Asey. "They've rung and rung, and they say the phone isn't out of order— The servants might not be home, but I'm sure Ty's father should be. Or his aunt. Or someone! And Ty ought to have been here hours ago— Oh, dear! Asey, shall we tell Father about the sail loft, and everything? I feel so criminal, not telling him, but on the other hand, I'm in such a confused state now, I'm beginning to wonder if I ever stumbled over that damned arm at all!"

Asey hesitated.

"I suppose," Jane went on, "there isn't any use telling people anyway, now, is there? It won't help. After all, there's nothing there!"

"S'pose," Asey said, "we keep this to ourselves for a while. Let's see what happens."

Back in the study, they found Nosey eating dog biscuit over the manuscript pages of the history of Quashnet on Charles Lennox's desk.

"It's a reward," Charles said. "He brought back the red wig. Here you are, Mayo."

Asey examined it.

"Looks like any other wig," Charles remarked. "I can't find any maker's name. Perhaps Nosey tore it off. He chewed through one part there, see? Nosey, where do you get these things, anyway?"

"Maybe it's better that you don't ever know," Jane said. "Dad, he's turning his limpid eyes on page sixty. Better rescue it."

Charles removed the manuscript. "Mayo, about Ethan Pilcher. D'you have that town record on—"

"No Quashnet, Dad," Jane said. "I can't stand any Quashnet right now."

"You *are* jumpy," her father said. "Look, neither of you got hurt, did you? You don't want a doctor to look you over? I have this feeling you're keeping things from me— Are you both really all right?"

Asey assured him that they were. "I didn't know," he added, "that you was a writer, Mr. Lennox."

Charles laughed. "It's not a generally accepted fact. You see, I retired last spring, rather suddenly. I'd been in the bank thirty years, and one morning I looked around at the people who'd been there more than thirty years, and I just took down my hat and cane, and retired."

Asey chuckled. "Decided you didn't want to be like the others, huh?"

"Exactly. People were aghast, and they told me I'd be bored, and regretful and back within three months. But you know, I never think of the bank except when they send me things to sign occasionally. And I'm having a wonderful time writing the history of Quashnet. If it's ever published, I'll probably be sued for libel. When I finish Quashnet, I'm going to write a novel on family life, and then I'm going to do a monograph on the hybrid spaniel," he pulled one of Nosey's ears, "and then I'm going to write a narrative poem about a bank president. Then — I think I hear a car outside."

Ten minutes later, Charles, Jane, Nosey and Asey set out in Asey's old roadster.

"Though why you call this old," Charles said, "I can't imagine. How'll we go about hunting this fellow, Asey? Where would you start hunting a man like Slocum?"

"We're not the only hunters in the field," Asey said, "an' my guess is that most of the obvious places've already been covered. But there's always back roads folks don't usually go on, an' they probably wouldn't think to look over. We'll try scourin' some of them."

He forgot that neither of his passengers was accustomed to his usual rate of speed, and he was too busy with his own thoughts to pay much attention to their reactions as the speedometer needle continued to slant.

They flew over back roads for half an hour without even seeing the headlights of another car.

When Asey finally slowed down to cross a main road, Charles Lennox reached across Jane and plucked mutely at Asey's coat sleeve.

"Er—did you see that strange figure back there?"

"What? Did you see someone? Whyn't you tell me? Where?"

"Frankly," Charles said, "I was so concerned with holding on, I couldn't speak. It was an odd, flapping sort of figure, Asey. Back beyond that junction of the two lanes."

Asey swung the roadster around in a manner which won Jane's admiration, and started back slowly over the road they had just traveled.

They found no trace of anyone, but on a parallel lane several minutes later, a man dashed toward them and waved frantically.

It turned out to be a state policeman, who thought they were Slocum and was infinitely annoyed when he discovered that they weren't. He went away muttering.

"Where's his motorcycle?" Jane asked.

"Beyond in the bushes," Asey said. "I think he was takin' a nap. Guess he feels the same way Jake did about this Slocum hunt. Well, we'll go back to town an' see if there's anything new."

Jane noticed, as they sped along Quashnet's Main Street, that the Bricker house was in darkness.

Cars were parked double all along the Shore Road, and up to the front steps of the brilliantly lighted new school.

"Looks like the whole township's there," Asey said. "Was Slocum goin' to make a political speech, or what?"

"Oh, you know how these things are," Jane said. "Supposedly civic, and not a bit partisan. But before the evening's over, everyone knows what lovely things you could do if you just happened to be elected to office. Uncle Jeff's a master of that sort of thing."

"I know. I've seen him turn a baked bean church supper into a rousin' rally," Asey said. "How's Jeff feel about this opposition?"

"It delights him," Charles said. "He hasn't been opposed for years, and he says it adds zest."

"You know how marvelous he looks in a cutaway?" Jane said. "Sort of gentleman-of-the-old-schooly? And you've seen him bound around kissing babies, and shaking hands, and telling stories? Well, of course, he makes Henry look like a tongue-tied hick, and Henry gets so embarrassed he starts knocking over water pitchers— Asey, you *know* we can't find him! What are we going to do?"

"I'm goin'," Asey stopped the car at the Shore Road gas station, "to make one last effort an' call my Cousin Syl Mayo."

"That funny little man with a walrus moustache? He fixes the Brickers' pump," Jane said. "Why call him?"

"Syl can find anythin'," Asey said. "He has a lost horse theory, an' it most always works."

"A what?"

"When Syl finds somethin'," Asey said, "an' you ask him how he done it, he says, 'Oh, it's like the feller that found the lost hoss. I just thought if I was a lost hoss where I'd go, an' I went there, an' it was.' I don't pretend to understand the inner workin's of the theory, but Syl gets results. If Syl can't find Slocum, Slocum can't be found!"

By the time Asey had succeeded in rousing his Cousin Syl from bed, cars were beginning to depart from the new school.

"We might as well go home," Jane said wearily, "and see what Mother's version is. Maybe she knows something."

They found Kate Lennox already seated in the living room when they returned to Cod Point.

Jefferson Gage was there, too, and Mrs. Lennox was giving him rather explicit directions about laying and lighting a fire in that particular fireplace.

They didn't either of them look, Asey thought, like people who had been having words with each other, as that cop said. They appeared to be on the friendliest of terms. And if either of them had been undergoing any nervous strain at Slocum's disappearance, neither showed it. Two more cheerful, tranquil people he had never seen.

"Dear child," Kate Lennox said to Jane, "*what* have you been doing to yourself? Look at your hands! And your face! And— Oh, it's Asey Mayo, isn't it?"

"He's been good enough to help us hunt Henry for you, Kate," Charles said. "Jeff, you know Asey, don't you?"

Jefferson Gage crossed the room and shook hands with Asey.

"Haven't seen you in a month of Sundays, Asey," he said. "Find any trace of Slocum?"

"No, but I just put Syl to work—"

"If anyone can find him," Jeff said, "Syl Mayo can! 'I thought if I was a hoss,' and so on! Kate, with the state police and Syl, you can't say we're not all doing our best!"

"You're all dears!" When Mrs. Lennox smiled, she didn't look much older than her daughter, Asey thought. "I didn't think Charles and Jane would be that interested. And Jeff's been wonderful, too. He did a magnificent, heroic thing, Charles. The most heroic—"

"Kate, don't!" Jeff protested. "You sound as if I'd been rescuing people from a burning tenement!"

"You did, practically. Charles, Jeff threw away his speech, and talked about Henry. He explained how Henry'd been called away to the bedside of a sick friend, and how his absence was going to give him an opportunity to say things he couldn't have said if Henry'd been there. Then he told about Henry's losing his family and having to go to work at fourteen, and how he'd worked his way along till he owned his own store, and how he'd taken night school courses to improve himself— Oh, Jeff was wonderful. He tied it up with the dedication by pointing out that the new school would make it possible for other Cape boys like Henry to get ahead in the world— Really, Jeff was wonderful! He was heroic!"

"I wasn't anything of the sort," Jeff said. "Asey'll assure you that praising your opponent lavishly under the circumstances was astute politics. After all, I'd have been a fool to run the boy down, wouldn't I?"

"Most people would have made cracks about Henry's not showing up," Kate said. "You *know* they would. But you saved his face, and mine. And the Governor was so impressed with the things Jeff said, he asked me to bring Henry to lunch with him next week. Jeff, you did a marvelous thing for the boy, and you saved his face."

Jeff Gage lighted a cigar, and sat down in front of the fire.

"I didn't do a thing for the boy, Kate. I was thinking solely of myself, and you. And after all that oratory, I need a drink. And some of your cheese, Charles. And Jane, you make some of those sandwiches I like. The kind with chives. I think I deserve a collation."

After the Lennox family hurried off to the kitchen, Jeff turned quickly to Asey.

"What's up, Asey? What's happened to Henry?"

"I don't know, Jeff. It's a funny situation. What do you think?"

"I don't understand it. Tonight was his big chance. I can't see why he wouldn't turn up, unless— D'you know him?"

"I seen his face on posters," Asey said. "That's all. I been too busy helpin' Bill Porter with cars to think much about politics. Besides, I always sort of take you for granted."

"Thanks." Jeff smiled, and then his face grew serious. "Asey, all the things I said tonight about Slocum are true. He was left an orphan without a penny, and by his own efforts, he's risen as high as he can go in this town. That's to his credit. That's admirable. That's the side of him Kate knows. But there are other sides Kate doesn't know, and I'd be the last one to tell her."

"Like what?"

"First there's his ambition. Kate thinks he wants to get elected so he can help Quashnet, but I know better. Slocum's ambition is for himself. He wants to be rich and powerful—that's natural, I grant you. And he discovered several years ago there was easy money and power too, in town jobs. He's been selectman, you know. He wants this seat of mine only for what he can get out of it. If it weren't for that, I'd step aside. I've had enough of politics. But I don't want that fellow to take my place, and I admit it frankly. That's why I'm humping myself this fall. I've picked up just enough about his future plans to know he'll undo in six months all my work of eighteen years."

"Mean to say he's planned some deals already?" Asey asked.

Jeff nodded. "In vino veritas. I've heard his friends bragging. They expect to flourish and grow fat on their cut from new state roads, and a town water system, and airports, and all. That leads to other sides, Asey. Slocum's a heavy drinker, and his friends aren't altogether laudable. He's cut both out to some extent since Kate took him in hand, because he's shrewd enough to realize the good Kate could do him. He's never let her find out anything to his disadvantage, and she's never guessed anything. His old friends are still with him, but I think that a few of them feel Henry's getting high hat and too good for 'em, and they're a little sore."

"Think they might be involved in this business?"

"I thought so at first," Jeff said, "and then as I watched 'em scurry around trying to find him tonight, I decided they weren't ready to tear up their meal ticket yet." Jeff paused. "And then there's one more side of Slocum that Kate doesn't know about. That's his tendency to run into girl trouble. When I found Slocum hanging around here so much, I set out to warn Charles about Jane. But I knew he'd lose that fiendish temper of his, and there was no telling what might happen. So I asked young Bricker to keep his eyes open."

"You don't think that perhaps Bricker an' Jane—" Asey left the question dangling.

"Oh, no. They've done some mad things, but Ty would have come to me if there'd been any trouble. But I have been wondering, Asey, if one of Slocum's romances might not have backfired on him tonight. I think there's a woman behind it. Well, anyway," Jeff said, "I've done my best to locate him, and I saved his face."

"An' gained much face by so doin'," Asey said.

Jeff smiled. "I've been in politics a good many years, Asey, and I think I can safely say that I know what the public likes. I try— Ah, food! Let's not mention politics till I've been satisfactorily fed. I missed my dinner, Aldrich was in such a hurry to get down here."

While they were eating, no one noticed the figure creeping along the hall outside. Even Nosey, asleep in front of the fire, ignored the intruder.

"Well," Kate Lennox said at last, "whatever's happened to Henry, he was saved tonight. And he's got the rally tomorrow to—"

"Yes, he has!"

Five pairs of eyes riveted on the figure that swayed in the doorway, a figure dressed in torn, filthy, flapping overalls.

"Good heavens!" Charles said. "That's what I saw on that back road. Why, it's Larrabee—I mean, Slocum!"

Slocum lurched into the room. He was accompanied by an overpowering aroma of whiskey.

"I been listening! I heard everything every one of you said since you came back! I know what happened now! It was all a plot! You pretended to be helping me," he pointed to Kate, "and all the time you was working for Gage! This is his plot!"

"You're drunk!" Jane said. "And you're crazy! Uncle Jeff *did* save your nasty face tonight! He gave an excuse for you, and he talked—"

"Yes!" Slocum said. "I heard! You had a hand in this, too, didn't you, Jane? All of you! All of you been plotting together, so Gage wouldn't get beaten! So I wouldn't win! You're the worst, Jeff Gage! You're behind this plot!"

"What plot?" Asey got up and walked over toward Slocum. The bulge in that overall pocket looked suspiciously like a gun. "What plot?"

"Keep away from me!" Slocum said. "Ask them what plot! They cooked it up!"

Kate Lennox found her voice. "Henry, you're drunk! Your big chance, the chance of your lifetime, and you went and got drunk!"

Jane, watching her mother's face, knew suddenly that what she had set out to achieve that evening had been accomplished. Henry Slocum was out of the Lennox family for good. In spite of all the mixup and the to-do, and the things that had happened and still weren't explained, she had won. Henry was out.

"I'm not drunk!" Slocum shouted. "Tomorrow morning, you'll find out how sober I am. I'm going to sue you for this, Gage. And tomorrow night at eight o'clock, I'm going to be at the rally at the school. You hear that? I'm going to be there, and I'm going to tell people what happened tonight! I'm going to expose this plot! I'm going to denounce you all!"

"Come on, Slocum!" Asey said. "Let's—"

Slocum pushed him away.

"Listen, Mayo! I'm going to be at that school tomorrow night, no matter what they try to do to keep me away! As long as I'm alive, I'll be there. Do you hear that?"

"They hear you in the next county, feller." Before Slocum realized what he was doing, Asey reached quickly into the overall pocket and removed a revolver. "Now, come on an' I'll take you home."

"Give me that gun!"

"Nope," Asey said. "This is enough, Slocum. Come along. I'll drive you home."

Slocum was trembling with fury. "I walked here, and I'll walk back! I—"

"Walked? Where's my car?" Jane demanded.

"You know where it is, all right. Get out of my way, Mayo!"

"Let him go," Jeff said quietly to Asey. "A good walk may cool him off."

"If you had your way, you'd cool me off!" Slocum said. "You'd kill me! You'll have to, if you want to keep me from exposing you tomorrow night at the rally!"

Slocum turned, and slammed out of the house.

It was after eleven o'clock the next night when Asey wearily walked up the path to the back door of his home in Wellfleet, after a solid day spent helping Sam repair the Porter.

He found four messages waiting for him on the kitchen table, telephone messages left by his Cousin Jennie before she went home.

All, he discovered, said the same thing.

"Slocum didn't come."

FIVE

ASEY sat at his breakfast table the following morning and watched his friend, Dr. Cummings, engage in his favorite indoor sport of baiting Lieutenant Hanson of the state police.

It was a little unfair of the doctor to be quite so caustic this morning, Asey thought, because Hanson had every right to be puzzled. Asey was puzzled himself.

He remarked as much to the doctor, who sniffed, and settled his rotund figure comfortably in the big easy chair.

"I'm not baiting the man, Asey. I just suggested in a friendly way that he ought to stop walking around the dining table in circles. He's getting dizzy. I simply told him I thought he ought to sit down, and relax, and listen. How does he expect to understand if he doesn't listen?"

"I *am* listening!" Hanson said. "But none of it makes any sense, anywhere! Asey, I can't make head nor tail of it all!"

"Give it to him again, Asey," Dr. Cummings said. "Begin at the beginning with you starting to try out the new car Thursday evening. No, on second thought, jump that part and start with Slocum leaving the Lennoxes' house, Thursday night. You got Slocum's movements up to there, Hanson?"

"No," Hanson said.

"Well, it was the night of the Quashnet school dedication, and Slocum was going to make a speech, but he never turned up, thereby causing a certain amount of consternation. Then, later, he appeared at the Lennoxes' on Cod Point, and said that he'd been the victim of a foul plot. There. Got that?"

"Why didn't he turn up at the school?" Hanson asked. "Where was he?"

"We don't know where he was. But he claimed that he had been the victim of a plot, and—"

"What was the plot?" Hanson interrupted.

"If there was a plot," Cummings said, "it was purely a figment of Slocum's imagination. It existed solely in Slocum's mind. Jeff Gage hadn't plotted to keep him away from the school. But events had apparently taken place which led Slocum to feel that there was a plot. In short, he was enjoying a delusion of persecution."

"What events?" Hanson asked. "What made him *think* there was a plot?"

"We don't know," Cummings said.

"Why didn't anyone find out? Asey, you were there, weren't you, when Slocum came? Why didn't you find out what'd happened to him?"

Asey smiled. "Slocum was in more of a denouncin' mood, Hanson, than an explainin' mood. He thought Jeff Gage an' the Lennox family was the ones that'd done things to him."

"Look," Cummings said, "d'you know Henry Slocum? Did you ever see him? You must have. He's one of the Quashnet selectmen."

"Tall, and dark? And a wide mouth?"

"With a lot of teeth. Yes. One of the brashest young men I ever met. Now when he came to the Lennoxes', he was reeking of whiskey—"

"But you said he wasn't drunk!"

"Hanson, don't get ahead of the story! Don't make things any harder! Get the picture, Hanson. Henry Slocum barged into the Lennox house in the middle of supper—"

"I thought it was eleven o'clock at night."

"Hanson," Cummings said patiently, "in some circles, a snack at that time is referred to as supper. The thing such people eat in the middle of the day is named luncheon, and the evening meal is—"

"Ssh, doc!" Asey said. "Hanson, when Slocum came in the living room, he was wearin' an undershirt an' a filthy pair of overalls, an' he was swayin', an' he smelled of whiskey. He reeked of it."

"Then he *was* drunk?"

"That was my feelin' at the time. I was just a little worried when I spotted a gun in his pocket—"

"What gun? You never said a thing about a gun before!" Hanson said unhappily. "What gun?"

"You wait a sec," Asey said, "an' I'll find it for you."

He left the room, and returned a few minutes later with a cheap, nickel plated revolver.

"Here. Heaven knows what'd have happened if he pulled the trigger," Asey said. "I don't think it's ever been cleaned. Now, let me get you straightened out, Hanson. When I saw Slocum in that condition, with this gun, I figured that he'd got cold feet at the thought of gettin' up before the Governor at this school dedication an' makin' a speech, an' he'd had a drink to brace him up, an' then he had another, an' another. Then I figured he'd pulled himself together enough to realize that he'd missed his speech, an' he wanted to blame someone, an' explain, an' in his muddled state, he come to the Lennoxes'. That's what I thought at first. See?"

"You thought he was drunk."

"Uh-huh. Then, as he talked on, I realized that he wasn't drunk, Hanson. He was shivering with the cold—mind you, he didn't have on any coat or overcoat. And he was so exhausted physically, he was swayin'. And he was so mad, he almost didn't know what he was doin' or sayin'. But he wasn't drunk."

"What about the smell? If he smelled—"

"Hanson," Cummings said, "a woman can smell of perfume and still not have been drinking it. You can smell of turpentine and still not be in the painting business. You can smell of ether without having undergone an operation! Be sensible, man! Slocum smelled of whiskey, but he wasn't drunk! He stood there ranting at Jeff Gage, practically launching the curse of Rome at him, and threatening all sorts of reprisals for this supposed plot, and then he slatted out. He refused to let Asey drive him home."

"Don't you think you should have insisted?" Hanson asked Asey. "With him in that state?"

"I don't see why." Cummings answered before Asey had a chance to open his mouth. "If Slocum was bent on walking the length of Cod Point Lane, and the length of the Bay Shore Road, why not let him? In the course of about the third mile, he ought to have cooled off."

"That's what Jeff Gage said," Asey told Hanson. "I thought so, too. He was too mad for anyone to try to reason with him, Hanson. As a matter of fact, he was so mad, I wouldn't have felt awful safe with him alone in the car. Anyway, Slocum stomped out, an' banged the door behind him."

"And vanished," Hanson said.

"No," Asey reached for his pipe, "he didn't vanish then. You see, I'd phoned for Syl to come over an' take a hand at findin' Slocum, an' Syl spotted him on Martin's Lane—that runs parallel to the Shore Road—an' followed him home. Syl spoke to him before he went into the house, and he claims that Slocum was sober, and calmed down— Jennie!" Asey raised his voice. "Jennie, what was it Slocum said to Syl?"

Jennie, his housekeeper cousin, bustled in importantly. She had kept the twenty-two line agog with her husband's findings in the affair of Henry Slocum.

"Syl, he asked if anything was wrong, and could he be of any help or anything, and Slocum shook his head—sad-like, Syl says. Then he said, 'No,

Syl—' You see, he knows Syl. Syl fixed his pump once. He said, 'No, Syl, I'm all right. Just leave me alone. I'm all right.' And Syl said Slocum sounded so unhappy, he asked him again if there wasn't something he could do. And Slocum said, 'No, Syl, I'm going to bed, and see if I can pick up the pieces tomorrow. I've been an awful fool.' An' then he went indoors."

"Didn't Syl ask what the matter was, or what had happened, or where Slocum had been?" Hanson demanded.

"He wanted to," Jennie said. " 'Course, if it'd been me, I'd have found out, all right! After all that to-do about him bein' lost! I'd just have kept on askin' questions till I found out every last thing. But Syl, he says he didn't want to have it seem he was pryin'. So he went back to his car, an' drove home, the dummy!"

Hanson thought for a moment.

"Did Syl tell you when he came home that he'd followed Slocum, and talked with him?"

Asey nodded. "He phoned an' told me, and I decided that whatever'd happened, Slocum realized he'd made a mistake blamin' Jeff an' the Lennoxes. So I called Jeff, an' he an' I decided that Slocum had seen the error of his way of thinkin', an' we thought the whole thing would blow over. You see, after the way Jeff covered up Slocum's absence at that school dedication business, an' the way Jeff talked of him, Slocum would only get in wrong by doin' anythin' against Jeff. See what I mean?"

"Yes," Hanson said. "Yes. But are you sure, Asey, that there *wasn't* some plot against Slocum?"

"Whatever happened," Asey said patiently, "Jeff and the Lennox family had nothing to do with it! Slocum thought so, but he was wrong!"

"The Lennoxes are rich, aren't they?" Hanson said. "And Jeff Gage has always had money, hasn't he?"

Dr. Cummings sighed.

"What's money got to do with it? Are you getting class conscious? If you had a highway accident involving a Ford and a Packard, would you automatically decide that the Packard driver was wrong, and the Ford driver was the victim of a plot? Please try not to be silly, Hanson! The Lennoxes and Jeff Gage are well to do, but you can hardly think of them as capitalists persecuting poor Henry Slocum!"

"I still think," Hanson said stubbornly, "if a man claims he's the victim of a plot, you ought to look into it!"

"Oh, my God!" Cummings said. "Are you way back there again? Look at it from another angle, can't you? A man, apparently drunk, storms into your house with a gun, and makes wild threats—"

"The Lennoxes ought to have called in the police," Hanson said. "If someone," he looked meaningly at Asey, "had called the police then, you wouldn't have Slocum vanishing into thin air! Vanished into thin air!"

"I'd love to have seen what you'd have done," Cummings said, "if the Lennoxes had happened to call you in on Thursday night! Look, Hanson, let's stop this quibbling and get on. Henry Slocum left the house at Cod Point, and went home, and went to bed, to all appearances a sadder and a wiser man. Then—"

"Then he vanished into thin air," Hanson said.

"You keep jumping ahead!" Cummings banged the arm of his chair in annoyance. "You keep leaping ahead, Hanson, and then you expect to understand what happened in between, and then you complain and say it's puzzling because things won't make sense!"

"Well, didn't he vanish?" Hanson persisted. "Didn't Slocum vanish into thin air? Nobody's laid eyes on him since Syl spoke with him Thursday night, have they? Hasn't Slocum vanished into thin air?"

"Sometimes, Hanson," the doctor said, "you

render me speechless! Sometimes I feel I have never known your equal for pure, solid, unadulterated thick-headedness. I know I've never seen your equal for taking the joy out of a narrative. If you refuse to listen to what has been painstakingly pieced together, how can you understand things? Now listen, Syl spoke with Slocum on Thursday night. And—"

"And nobody's seen Slocum since! And what I can't understand," Hanson said, "is why Asey, or somebody, didn't have sense enough to look into things right then, on Thursday night! Here's a man claims he's the victim of a plot, and nobody lifts a finger to do anything about it! You just let him go off into the night! Nobody checks up to see if he's all right. Nobody tries to find out what happened to him Thursday night that he didn't make his speech! Nobody lifts a finger! And now he's disappeared into thin air—"

"If I hear that phrase again," Dr. Cummings said, "I shall become violently ill. Hanson, I keep trying to explain to you that if you'd just relax, and listen, you'd understand. Now, you don't take the threats of a drunk very seriously, do you?"

"But you said he wasn't drunk and—"

"No, he wasn't drunk! But you don't take threats seriously when they're made by a man as furious as Slocum was, either. To all intents and purposes, the man was out of his head with rage. Now, when Syl saw him, Slocum was calmed down. He wanted to be left alone, and to go to bed. He'd made a fool of himself, and he was going to try to set things right the next day—"

"Why didn't anyone go to *see* him the next day?" Hanson demanded.

"If you'd listened," Cummings said, "you would understand that as far as the general public was concerned, Henry Slocum had gone off on an errand of mercy. Jeff Gage explained Slocum's absence from the school dedication by saying he'd gone to the bedside of a sick friend. The general public had been told that on Thursday night, and they believed it, and they had no reason to seek Slocum out on Friday morning."

"But Asey knew different," Hanson said. "So did Jeff Gage and Mrs. Lennox."

"Yes, and so did some of Slocum's friends. And so did three of your colleagues that Jeff Gage sent out to hunt Slocum Thursday night. They all knew, but they were the only ones who did. Now, after Jeff Gage announced the sick friend business, Slocum's pals realized that he'd saved the situation for Slocum, and that there wasn't much need for them to keep up their frantic hunt—"

"How do you know that?" Hanson asked.

"I talked with a couple of 'em last night," Asey said. "They got tired huntin' him, an' they knew he could always say his piece at the rally the next night. That is, last night. An' they figured, too, that maybe Jeff had done a better job for Slocum than Slocum might have done for himself. Like one of the fellers said, you couldn't tell but what Slocum might have got stage fright in front of the Governor, an' made a mess of things. An' the way Jeff put it, Slocum's not bein' there made a good impression. Made it seem like a sick friend was more important to Slocum than politics was. So Slocum's pals called it a day, an' went down to Provincetown an' finished up the night at the Gypsy Tea Room and Bar."

"That reminds me," Hanson said, "we got to raid that joint again soon. But look here, didn't any of Slocum's friends go over to see if he was home yesterday?"

"After their night at the Gypsy Tea Room an' Bar," Asey said, "Slocum's pals didn't feel much like makin' any social calls till yesterday afternoon. Even last night, the boys were still lookin' considerable peaked."

"But—"

"You see, Hanson," Cummings cut off Hanson's protest, "why no one bothered much about Slocum yesterday is really very simply explained. His friends were recovering from hangovers. Your three cops had gone along back to Boston with the Governor Thursday night—from what Asey said, I gather they hadn't taken a very vigorous interest in the Slocum hunt, anyway. As far as the rest who knew were concerned—I mean Jeff, and Asey, and the Lennoxes—why, they knew Slocum went penitently to bed Thursday night, and they thought that everything would be cleared up on Friday morning."

"Why didn't any of 'em *do* something about it yesterday morning?" Hanson said. "Why didn't you at least go over, Asey, and sort of make sure that things *would* be cleared up?"

"Well," Asey said, "I called Jeff up yesterday mornin', an' asked him if he thought we'd better do anything. We talked it over, an' decided we'd better let Slocum make the first move. We thought Slocum would apologize to Mrs. Lennox, an' smooth things over, because it was to his advantage to apologize to her an' do some smoothin'. We both thought it'd be best to wait an' let him take the initiative. We thought that proddin' him might not be the wisest course. So I went over to Sam's an' looked at my smashed-up car—"

"You mean, you put the whole affair right out of your mind?" Hanson asked.

Asey nodded. "An' I found my car wasn't hurt so bad, so I drove up to Boston, an' got some parts, an' come back, an' worked on the car with Sam till his wife made him come home to bed. That's how I spent my day. An' the Lennoxes an' Jeff, they sat around twiddlin' their fingers all day, waitin' for Slocum to show up."

Hanson shook his head. "Well, I suppose you all *thought* you were doing the right thing. You say his friends went to Slocum's house yesterday afternoon?"

"The two Collins fellers went, an' found Slocum gone, an' his sedan gone from the barn, so—"

"Wait," Hanson said, "what ever became of the Lennox girl's Porter that he had?"

"That was Thursday that Slocum had the Porter," Cummings said. "Thursday! Asey is now talking about yesterday afternoon. Friday afternoon—"

Cummings launched into a caustic little monologue on what had happened Thursday, what had happened Friday, and how, if Hanson would only listen, Hanson might conceivably understand the course of action.

Ordinarily, Asey would have interrupted the

doctor's digression, but at the moment he was rather relieved to have the subject of Jane's roadster sidetracked. He had seen Jane whizzing by in it earlier that very morning in Quashnet, but he had no knowledge of how she'd got the car back, or where it had been found. And he didn't want to go into the matter with Hanson just then. There was nothing to be gained by letting Hanson form premature theories about Jane.

"Got the time settled now? Good," Cummings said. "The Collins boys thought Slocum had gone out, so they went back home and had another nap. Slocum's clerk opened up Slocum's store yesterday morning, but he didn't think it unusual that Slocum didn't put in an appearance. He thought Slocum was still away with a sick friend. Other friends of Slocum's came to his house during the afternoon, but they thought he was just out somewhere. Nobody really worried about him till he didn't appear at the rally last night."

"Why didn't Jeff Gage call you right away?" Hanson demanded. "Why'd he wait so long?"

"There was a lot of odds an' ends of speakers first," Asey said. "Then Jeff, an' finally Slocum, separated by a band concert. Jeff thought Slocum was goin' to wait till that was over, an' then come at the last minute. When he didn't, Jeff told Art

Collins to announce that Slocum was delayed coming back to town, an' then Jeff phoned here an' left a message for me—"

"Certainly made a big effort, didn't he?" Hanson said. "Phoned and left a message! Why didn't he hunt you up?"

"Well, Hanson, he couldn't leave the rally to come over here. What with one candidate missin', Jeff had to sort of stick around. An' the Lennoxes had set out on another Slocum hunt. So Jeff left the message with Jennie. She tried to get me at Sam's but we'd got so tired of Sam's wife callin' him up, we'd just disconnected the phone. When I come back home here, an' found the messages, I tried to phone Jeff, an' finally I drove over an' located him. Then he an' I phoned you— Did it take you long to get his description an' license plate numbers out over the teletype an' the radio?"

"They were all over New England in fifteen minutes," Hanson said. "Asey, if you'd told me more about this last night, I'd have come right down here with some men! If you'd only told me that he told you that he'd be at the rally if he was alive, I'd have brought the whole outfit down last night!"

"And just what good would that have done?" Cummings wanted to know. "What could you have done? Nothing, absolutely nothing! The only thing you could do was what Asey phoned you to do—send out his description and car license plate numbers, and see if anyone had seen him or his car. You couldn't jump to any conclusions about foul play till you'd made a pretty good effort to locate him and his car, could you?"

"We could have started in just that much earlier to find out who kidnapped him, couldn't we?" Hanson retorted.

"Who," Cummings said, "ever muttered that ugly word? Who ever said anything about a kidnapping? Where did you get the quaint notion that Slocum has been kidnapped?"

"Listen," Hanson said, "we can't find any trace of him or his car. If he's dead, we ought to find his corpse and his car, oughtn't we? And if he's alive, we ought to find someone who saw him or his car, somewhere, oughtn't we? So what have you got left? You got what he told you himself. You got a plot, haven't you? And if you can't find him alive or dead, then it's a kidnap plot, isn't it?"

Cummings sighed.

"You sound just like that violet soap mystery program that my wife listens to. 'Is Slocum really the victim of a kidnap plot? Is Slocum really dead?

Is Slocum really alive? Listen in tomorrow at the same time, and see what has become of Slocum!' The victim of a kidnap plot! Oh, my God!"

"That's all right!" Hanson said angrily. "He said there was a plot to keep him away from the school dedication, didn't he? He told Asey if he was alive, he'd be at the rally last night, didn't he? But he wasn't, was he? So I say, he's been kidnapped! And I'm going to find—"

"P'raps," Asey said, "you better sit down an' listen to the rest of the story, Hanson. There's some more."

Cummings grinned. "Going to tell him what happened to you Thursday night after your car got smashed up? About the sail loft, and all? Ah!" He sat back expectantly and lighted a fresh cigar. "Hanson's going to like this!"

Briefly and succinctly, Asey summed up the events of Thursday evening. He told of Jane's stumbling over the limp arm in the tweed sleeve, of Nosey's finding the red wig, of his chasing the stranger with the felt hat and the turned-down brim.

And it still, Asey thought as he talked on, sounded plumb crazy!

"That," he wound up, "is what happened to me Thursday night, Hanson."

"Want him to go over it four or five times more, Hanson?" Cummings inquired.

But Hanson seemed to have grasped the story with the first telling.

"I thought there was more to this than you let on at first, Mayo! I thought you were holding things back! I—"

"I wasn't holdin' 'em back," Asey protested. "I was just tryin' to give you the story in some sort of order. I—"

"You know what I think?" Hanson said furiously. "I think you're getting too high-handed for your own good, Mayo. There isn't any reason for you to take matters into your own hands, as if you were the law! Why didn't you report this to me? A girl falls over a corpse, and you don't say a word about it— I suppose you thought you'd solve it all by yourself, huh?"

"There *wasn't* any corpse," Asey said gently.

"Ever since you had your picture on that news magazine cover," Hanson went on, "you've felt pretty damn big, haven't you? Why didn't you report these things to me, I'd like to know?"

"Wa-el," Asey drawled a little, "when I got to the sail loft, there wasn't any corpse, or any sign of one. Jane found a flask she said was Slocum's, an' she thought the tweed was like Slocum's coat.

But Slocum turned up as alive as could be, an' he was the only person that seemed to be missin'. I decided maybe the girl might have stumbled over him, an' then he'd shed the coat later. Or she might have stumbled over a tramp. But no matter how you figger, Hanson, there wasn't any corpse to report to you!"

"You ought to have reported the whole thing!"

"But be reasonable, Hanson!" Asey said. "A dog findin' a red wig isn't anythin' to complain about to the police! An' as for the feller in the dark felt hat with the turned-down brim—well, a tourist once spent a whole night skulkin' around my orchard on the chance of hearin' a bird sing. Jennie found a stranger lurkin' in back of her barn in July, an' he turned out to be a Harvard professor waitin' for the right kind of moonlight to take a candid camera view of the silo an' the old outhouse. The feller I chased might have been guilty of trespass, Hanson, but it wasn't anything to call you for!"

Hanson got to his feet.

"You think I'm pretty dumb, don't you, Mayo? You and Cummings think I'm dumb! You—"

"Now, now, Hanson!" the doctor said, "don't ask for it!"

"You listen to me, you two! Before I came to

this house this morning, I went over to Quashnet. And I asked questions. I asked a lot of questions. And I found out that Jeff Gage had said some very interesting things about Slocum. He said he was going to keep Slocum from getting his seat and winning the election if it was the last thing he ever did!"

"Uh-huh," Asey said. "I know. Jeff told me that Thursday night. He's never made any secret of wanting to beat Slocum."

"All right! Who benefits most by Slocum's not turning up at the school, and at this rally? Jeff Gage! Who's got a motive for getting Slocum in wrong, and discrediting him? Gage! Who else would want to keep Slocum from speaking, and from rallies, and all that? Who else but—"

"Let me guess," Cummings said. "Jeff Gage! So what are you going to do, Hanson, arrest Jeff Gage? Oh, that'll be peachy fun! What'll you arrest him for? Conspiracy to help an opponent by saving his face? Conspiracy to help find a missing opponent? Cons—" He broke off as the telephone rang. "If that's my wife, Asey, tell her I've left for the hospital."

Asey grinned as he picked up the receiver, and then he passed it to Hanson.

"For you."

Both Asey and Cummings looked studiedly at the rug, and tried not to listen to the conversation that followed. But they heard enough to take the edge off Hanson's triumphant announcement as he hung up.

"I was going to tell you that I'd put two men to work watching Jeff Gage. And now it looks like I was right when I thought they'd probably find out what'd become of Slocum."

Hanson paused.

"Oh, get on! Don't try to be dramatic!" Cummings said. "Say it! We've guessed, anyway. They've found Slocum's body!"

"That's only half of it." Hanson's smile was almost a smirk. "Gage and the Lennox girl have just taken Slocum's body from the Lennoxes' sail loft, and loaded it into the back of the Lennox girl's roadster. And now they're headed for the back shore with it."

SIX

"THEY'RE on that road over towards Austin's Hollow," Hanson continued. "Bradley's following 'em in the car, and Pat stopped off to phone me. Looks like we got 'em with the goods."

"Looks," Asey said, "like you have."

Hanson strutted to the dining room doorway, then he turned and smiled at the doctor.

"Not just a kidnap plot, doc, but a kidnap plot with a dash of murder. I haven't got room in my car to take you two, but you can see the finale if you want to."

He put on his cap with a flourish, and strode out to his coupé.

"Asey," Cummings pitched his cigar stub into the fireplace, "did you hear what I just heard? Jeff Gage, and Jane Lennox—with Slocum's body?"

"Yup, I heard."

"Jeff, and that girl!" Cummings shook his head. "If that's so, then Hanson's got a right to smirk and strut— But it can't be true, Asey! There's something wrong somewhere. This can't be. It isn't possible!"

"It don't seem possible," Asey agreed. "On the other hand, doc, Hanson's men wouldn't invent a yarn like this. I guess maybe perhaps you an' I had better meander over to the hollow, doc, an' sort of take a look into things. Come on."

Outside, Cummings viewed Asey's new Porter with some alarm.

"What's happened to the side of the thing? It looks dissected!"

"Oh, it's just stripped a bit," Asey said. "I got some new fenders and stuff comin'. She looks a little naked, but she goes all right— Don't lean on that door, doc. The catch don't work."

"Suppose the door opens while we—"

"It won't if you don't lean on it. Get in, doc, an' stop lookin' worried. Hustle."

The doctor hesitated, but his curiosity as to what might be going on at the hollow overcame his suspicions about the efficiency of the patched-up car. He got in, and, as they started off, shut his eyes tight. He knew from long experience that was the only restful way to ride with Asey Mayo.

"Some fine day, Asey," he observed after a minute or two, "I'm going to get a call to sweep your mangled remains out of a ditch into a dustpan. This infernal machine feels as if it went even faster than the others."

"Don't you ever get tired of that dustpan notion, doc? You been airin' that for so many years, I— Well, well. Look what we got!"

Cummings opened his eyes as the car braked.

They had pulled up alongside a police car with a flat tire.

"Hi, Bradley," Asey said to the officer struggling with the jack. "Run into some trouble?"

"Trouble? You see that glass?" Bradley pointed to the fragments strewn over the road. "You know what happened, Asey? That girl with Jeff, she pitched two bottles out of her car, and they smashed, and when I drove along—bang! If you're after Hanson, he's gone on to the shore."

"Where's Pat?"

"With Hanson. Hanson picked him up in the village. I was following along after Gage and that Lennox girl— Say, did you know they got Slocum's body? Did Hanson tell you?"

Asey nodded.

"You could have knocked me over with a feather," Bradley said, "when I saw the two of 'em cart that body out from that sail loft. I almost dropped my binoculars. I guess it just goes to show you can't tell about people, can you? I thought Hanson was crazy when he said for us to watch Gage— If Hanson asks, tell him I'll be right along."

Cummings looked at Asey as he steered the car around the glass, and drove on.

"Asey, maybe I'm being dull—but is it possible that cop meant that Jane Lennox deliberately threw bottles on the road to keep him from following her and Gage?"

"Seems," Asey said, "like she an' Jeff are just cuttin' loose, don't it?"

"Apparently," Cummings said, "when law abiding citizens cut loose, they remember all the things they saw in gangster movies. Think of that lovely looking girl racing away with a corpse in her rumble seat! Think of her hurling bottles so the broken glass would foil pursuing cops! I think this is incredible."

Asey parked on the turntable at the end of the road, and then he and the doctor walked through the coarse sea grass in the hollow between the dunes to the beach beyond.

Jeff Gage, his arm hooked in Jane's, stood by a clump of seaweed where the sand began to slant down to the breaking surf.

Both appeared to be shaking with laughter.

After the doctor and Asey walked nearer, they found out why.

Jeff and Jane were watching the antics of Hanson and his trooper, who were trying to lay their hands on a body that bobbed tantalizingly out of their reach just beyond the breakers. The body would poise on the crest of a wave, and then, as the wave curved to break, the body would bobble back and float to meet the next incoming breaker.

Both men were drenched to the armpits, and both were loudly disagreeing on the method of getting the body to shore.

Jane and Jeff chortled as Hanson fell flat in the undertow.

"Well!" Dr. Cummings said, "I must say that neither of you looks as lawless as you've been sounding. I don't know whether to be relieved, or appalled at your callousness."

"Oh, hello, doctor!" Jeff said genially. "Hello, Asey! Didn't hear you come. Have you seen our struggling friends? Think they'll get it?"

Jane greeted Asey with a radiant smile.

"Asey, we've had more fun! And the cops chased us! And Uncle says they'll probably arrest me for collusion or something, because I dropped two bottles of Mother's cleaning fluid stuff on the road. It was purely an accident, I just turned around to see if we really were being followed, and the bottles slipped off the boot, and broke, and that cop got a flat— D'you think they'll get mad, Asey?"

"I sort of think," he told her, "that they are."

"It's ridiculous!" Jane said. "It was an accident— Oh, Hanson's fallen again!"

Asey watched for a moment beside her, and then he strolled down the slanting shore to the edge of the waves rolling up.

Then he returned, grinning, and devoted himself to enjoying the scene.

"This reminds me," Dr. Cummings said happily, "of the old Mack Sennett days. This is more like Mack Sennett than anything I've seen in years. I shouldn't be at all surprised to see those two start throwing custard pies at each other, any minute. My, my, I wish this retrieving epic could be viewed by a larger audience. This is something that shouldn't be missed!"

None of it was being missed by the man lying in the tall sea grass of the dune behind them. He was muttering to himself as he grimly watched the struggles of Hanson and the trooper, and his clenched fist ground into the dry white sand.

He showed himself for a second as a gust of wind blew off his dark felt hat. But he grabbed his headgear before it could get away, and crouched back in the grass, and continued his grim watching.

"Where'd you get this body, Jeff?" Asey asked at last.

"Oh, some of my boys had it for a crowning gesture to the rally last night. They were all set for an old time rally, with red fire and a comb band and all, it seemed. I'd heard rumors of this, but when Slocum didn't turn up, I told the boys they had better take it away."

"How'd it get in the sail loft?"

"The boys asked where to put it, and I said the loft. It was the first place that entered my mind, I don't know why. And then this morning when Jane came over, she and I decided we'd better get rid of it. It would simply have been horseplay to drag it around at the rally under ordinary circumstances, but it didn't seem to be the ideal thing for the police to stumble on this morning. So we loaded it into her car to bring it over here and cast it to the waves, and," Jeff laughed, "do you know what I think, Asey? I think Hanson's got men trailing me!"

"I know he has," Asey said. "Hanson's decided that of all the people in the world, you got the finest motives for disposin' of Henry Slocum. The doc an' I went over the whole business with Hanson this mornin', step by step, an' it sort of pains me to tell you that Hanson's decided that you've kidnapped Slocum. That's his conclusion."

"You're joking!"

"Until Hanson's thought of someone better," Asey said, "you're suspect number one. I was goin' to warn you."

"But that's the silliest thing I ever heard in my life!" Jeff looked incredulous. "Me? *Me!*"

"Yup. You. An' if I was you, Jeff, I'd kind of watch out that I didn't irritate him too much. I know you can bust him with a flick of your wrist, but Hanson's an earnest, honest feller, an' the reporters know it."

Jeff nodded slowly. "I see what you mean."

"I thought you would," Asey said. "Without bein' too obvious, I think maybe I'd give Hanson a detailed report of my life for the past few days, if I was you. Didn't you drive down with the Governor on Thursday? Well, tell him that, in passin'. Tell him who you lunched with yesterday—"

Jeff laughed. "I lunched with his boss!"

"Tell him, an' give him the menu. Hanson isn't really as dumb as the doc likes to pretend. He's a good, routine man. But like I tell the doc, you shouldn't expect Einstein for the salary that Hanson gets. I— Hey, they got it!"

Hanson and Pat, dripping from head to foot, dragged ashore the figure, which promptly collapsed and left Hanson holding one of the arms.

"That's a pretty good dummy," Jeff said critically. "Jabez Craddock's work. He used to make scarecrows by the dozen in the old days—remember 'em? Always had a red necktie."

"Didn't he do Santa Clauses?" Cummings asked.

"Still does. Nickerson always has one of Jabe's Santas in his store window at Christmas. They tell me he does better Hitlers than he did Kaisers. This Slocum was pretty good. He made the teeth out of wood, and he got that rift in the front. It's probably primitive of me," Jeff added, "but I like dummies, and sometimes it's given me pleasure to see my opponents hanged in effigy. Now, all of you help me with Hanson. Hear that, Jane? No cracks, and you *grovel* about that cleaning fluid, young woman! We've got to salve him and soothe his spirits."

Jeff walked forward to meet the dripping Hanson.

"He'll do it, too," Cummings said. "He'll have Hanson eating out of his hand. You know, Miss Lennox, I've got only one thing against your uncle. His shirts."

"Uncle has lovely shirts!" Jane said. "I was just thinking, he's the only well-dressed man in the family. Dad's so lank, his clothes always seem to trail behind him, and he stuffs his pockets so full of junk that he gets things out of shape. And Emmet's just sloppy. What's the matter with Uncle's shirts, doctor?"

"My wife."

"What?"

"My wife," Cummings said, "doesn't see why mine won't fit like Jeff's. That's why she always votes for him. She likes his shirts. I'm so tired of hearing about Jeff's shirts—"

"Doctor," Jeff came up with his arm hooked firmly through Hanson's, "will you be good enough to see that the lieutenant and his trooper won't suffer from their—er—ducking? I'm taking them to my house, and they can get baths, and dry clothes, and a drink, but I'd like you to go over them just to make sure."

Asey stepped on Cummings's foot.

"Glad to, Jeff, glad to!" the doctor said hastily. "Glad to! Er—sure."

"I'll drive 'em over," Asey said. "I can get 'em there in five minutes. Hot bath an' a drink first, doc?"

"Yes, and I'll come and thump you— Who's going to drive me, you, Miss Lennox? Well, I'll thump you as soon as she gets me there. Can't be too care-

ful, and all that. Matter of fact," the doctor re-
verted to his usual caustic form, "matter of fact,
Hanson, I can't see why you should dash into the
ocean like that just to pull out a dummy, on a chilly
day with an east wind—"

"All my fault, doctor," Jeff said hurriedly. "I
didn't explain things sufficiently. You see, Jane and
I had just thrown it in when the lieutenant came,
and when he asked if it were Slocum, I said yes.
And the lieutenant's just explained to me about a
case he had once where a genuine body was made
to look like a dummy. It's all a perfectly natural
but unfortunate misunderstanding, as the Governor said to me when we were driving down
Thursday night, apropos of— Come, come, we must
get along! You're shivering! Ready, Asey?"

Cummings watched a little wistfully as Jeff
walked off with Hanson and Asey and the trooper.

"You know, Miss Lennox," he said, "with a manner like your uncle's, a general practitioner—even
an average general practitioner—could afford shirts
like your uncle's. Let's get along— Say, look up
there! Did you see something move on the dune?"

"Newspaper," Jane said. "See? It's blowing
down the side. Are you getting that way too, seeing
things moving all over the place and wondering
if it's Henry Slocum? Dad cut himself shaving, this

morning. He thought he saw a man in the rhododendrons. Well, let's get along!"

Asey was waiting outside Jeff Gage's home on the Shore Road in Quashnet when Jane drove up with her uncle and the doctor.

"Okay? Sure, they're okay," Asey said in answer to Jeff's question. "They're never goin' to get over your plumbin' fixtures in a million years, either. Doc, don't you dare let loose at Hanson till Jeff gets off the suspect list. I'll either wait for you an' drive you to the hospital, or have Sam bring your car here for you—which?"

"I'm always happier in my own vehicle. I grant you it won't do over forty, but the doors close. I'll phone Sam."

Jane started to follow Jeff and the doctor indoors, but Asey stopped her.

"Want a few words with you, youngster. I noticed you didn't have your roadster last night—when'd you get it back?"

"Oh, I was with the family in the sedan last night. We were showing off for Uncle's sake at the rally. We had William drive. Dad didn't want him, but Mother insisted, and said we must, and Dad said we just looked foolish because William hasn't a proper uniform and his cap's too small. It belonged to the man before William, and Mother won't get another because she says it's almost new. So—"

"Stop bein' glib, now," Asey said. "When'd you get your roadster back?"

"Thursday."

"Thursday?"

"Yes. Thursday night."

"You didn't have it when I left your house Thursday night!" Asey said.

"It was in the garage," Jane told him, "on Thursday night. I didn't know it was there. I didn't find it till yesterday when I went out to get the beach-wagon. But William and Mary say it was in the garage when they came home Thursday night."

"Who brought it back?"

Jane shrugged.

"Ty, maybe?" Asey asked.

"Ty's gone to New York with his father. He went Thursday—that's why he didn't turn up at the sail loft. His father had a phone call about business, and he rushed out and grabbed Ty and had Ty drive him over. Ty called up from New York yesterday and explained. He was sore, because he didn't want to go to New York, but after I'd told him what'd gone on, he decided it was a stroke of luck for us."

Asey looked at her searchingly.

"Don't you believe me?" Jane demanded. "Dear me, Asey, haven't we gone over that Coast Guard and African chant business enough? Here's Uncle— Uncle Jeff, will you please come here and tell Asey that Ty Bricker went to New York Thursday with his father, and he's still there?"

"That's true, Asey," Jeff said. "Jane, you and I went rushing off so impulsively after that dummy when you came earlier, I completely forgot to ask how your mother is. Is Kate taking it easy, as she promised me?"

"Well," Jane said, "she hunted Slocum practically all night. She and I. And poor William. He had to change a tire on the East Pochet swamp road, and something hideous happened to the ignition on that clay road going to the dyke. It wasn't a restful outing, at all."

"We really ought to have organized things," Jeff said regretfully. "Garfield and I covered the swamp and the dyke, too."

"You mean you went huntin', Jeff, last night after I left you?" Asey asked.

Jeff nodded. "I had Garfield drive me around for a while. And some of my boys were out. It occurred to me it would be rather fun if our side were the ones to rescue him from a mud hole, or something. Jane, I'm worried about your mother and the way she's wearing herself out over all this. Can't your father *do* anything?"

"You know Mother when her mind's made up," Jane said. "Nobody can do much. Dad made us take him home around two last night. He went to bed. He said he was tired of hunting Slocum, and anyway, if he were the fellow, he'd seek out a sick friend and sit by his bedside. Dad said that would solve everything, and torment us to boot. Mother was still in bed when I left the house this morning, and Dad swore he'd try to keep her there."

"How does Mrs. Lennox feel about this?" Asey asked.

"She's got a look in her eyes that says she's going to find him—"

"I mean, how does she feel about Slocum, himself?"

"I haven't dared go into that very deeply," Jane said. "But I'm convinced she's undergone a pretty complete reversal of feeling about him. She feels he let her down, and that he threw away his big chance, and she resents it after all her efforts with his speech, and all the rest. I think if he'd really been drunk, she'd have excused him and passed it off, don't you, Uncle?"

Jeff nodded. "I think she'd have passed it off, anyway, if he hadn't gone into that plot business so strongly. It was one thing for Slocum to let her down, but it was something different for him to accuse the lot of us of conspiring against him. That was where Slocum made his mistake, because your mother has a very firm family feeling."

"Dad confided to me," Jane said, "that he thinks Mother's real reason in trying to find Slocum now is to make him eat his words about us. I think there's a lot in that."

"Tell me," Asey said, "has she got any theories as to what's happened to him?"

Jane and Jeff exchanged a grin.

"Mother's run the gamut, Asey," Jane said. "Beginning with amnesia. She's thought of every conceivable thing that could happen to him, from his getting his foot caught in a bear trap to being sucked into the mud of the East Pochet swamp. We've covered every sensible angle, and a lot that Father thought up. My only hope is that if he hasn't been found, he must be alive."

"Asey," Jeff said, "what about this sail loft business—all the to-do that you and Jane had Thursday night?"

Asey shrugged.

"As far's we know, Slocum was the only one missin' then, an' he turned up okay. So—"

"No!" Jane said vehemently. "No more sail loft!

I want to forget it. Nosey's made off with the red wig, and Mother threw the flask away in a fit of temper, and now I'm trying to put the rest out of my mind just as completely. I practically had it all obliterated yesterday, but now it's coming back and haunting me at intervals— Uncle, haven't you any work that I can do? Something so I'll stop thinking about Henry Slocum, and worrying about— Oh, I don't know what the worst is, but I wish it would happen and get this foul suspense over with! Uncle, can't I balance your check book or do the house accounts, or sort the sheets, or something? I did everything like that at our house yesterday."

"Over at headquarters," Jeff told her, "are boxes of envelopes waiting to be addressed. Into each one you slip a blue blotter with a picture of me beaming, and a lapel button with a profile of me, also beaming. I can keep you busy for a week. If you'll come in and wait till I put the finishing touches on Hanson, you can drive me over to headquarters, too. Then Garfield can take Hanson and his trooper back in the Cadillac. D'you think the mink lap robe would be going too far, Asey?"

"I think that town car of yours'll be enough," Asey said. "I told you, the plumbin's already stunned 'em."

"Wait," Jeff said, "till they spot the clothes I'm

going to lay out for 'em. Asey, you've been awfully decent, and I appreciate it. From now on, I'm going to have a thousand witnesses to every move I make, just in case anyone else starts in entertaining base suspicions. I'm going to sit in the window at headquarters in full view of the public, beaming."

He returned to the house, but Jane lingered behind.

"Asey."

"Yup?"

"Asey— Oh, this is going to sound so damn silly!"

"Go on," Asey said encouragingly. "What's on your mind?"

"Last night at the rally, there was a man with a turned-down dark felt hat. He was way in the back of the hall, and I couldn't see his face, but I kept thinking of that man you chased. And—and this morning, Dad thought he saw a man with a felt hat in the rhododendrons. It— Oh, it just seems so damn silly to tell you things like this!"

"I dunno," Asey said, "as it does. Anythin' else?"

"It *is* silly!" Jane insisted. "It just goes to show you the state of mind we're all in— Think of Dad cutting himself shaving, because he thinks he sees a man in the bush. After all, as you said about the tweed sleeve, there are hundreds of tweed coats like Slocum's in Wellfleet, or any other town. I suppose there are untold hordes of men with dark hats and turned-down brims."

"True," Asey said. "But—"

"And, of course," Jane went on, "there's no reason why there shouldn't be strangers at the rally. And as Dad said, those surveyors for the new road are wandering around all over the place. One of 'em trampled the asparagus bed to pieces only last week. Said he thought it was just weeds! And— Oh, Asey, I can't reassure myself, though! I keep having that feeling I had in the sail loft the other night, of something evil and sinister going on! Everything's all right on the surface, but my spine keeps shivering!"

"Seen this feller any other times or any other places?" Asey asked. "Or is there anythin' else that happened an' worried you?"

"Everything worries me!" Jane said. "We're all worried, Mother and Dad and Jeff and I. Mother forgot to make out the grocery list and the week-end order— That sounds trivial enough, but as Mary said this morning, it never happened before in the two years she's worked for us. And did you notice that Uncle Jeff had on one pigskin glove stitched with brown, and one stitched with black? He had the right and left all right but they weren't mates. That sounds trivial, too, but for him it's practically an upheaval. It's catching, this worry is. Why, over at the back shore this morning, Dr. Cummings jumped at a piece of newspaper blowing down the side of the dunes! Asey, what *is* going on?"

"I don't know any more'n you do, youngster. Huh."

He started to walk over toward his car.

"Where are you going?" Jane asked.

"I think I'll drive over to Slocum's house an' do some prowlin' before Hanson gets there. My cousin Syl was goin' to snoop around, too, and I want to see if he's found anythin' out."

"Asey, you will be careful, won't you? Have you got a gun?"

Asey grinned at her solicitous tone. "Not with me, no."

"I thought you always carried a Colt! It says so in the papers. A big old Colt that barks."

"This mornin'," Asey said, "I set out to investigate a corpse bein' thrown away into the broad Atlantic by two supposedly reputable people. It didn't seem necessary to lug along any ole barkin' Colts. You be careful yourself, youngster, an' if you spot ole turned-down brim, don't sing any African chants. Call out the Coast Guard instead."

He got into the roadster and drove away.

At the junction of the Shore Road and the road that led to the village, Asey hesitated and finally came to a dead stop.

Perhaps it wouldn't be such a bad idea if he drove home and picked up a gun before he did any snooping at Slocum's house. Because, when he drove Hanson and Pat from the back shore, he had been almost certain that he saw a man on the big dune at Austin's Hollow. He hadn't given it any particular thought at the time. More often than not, there were people at the hollow, bass fishermen or people on beach picnics, or just ordinary tourists watching the surf.

But now in the light of Jane's tidings about the man at the rally and the man in the rhododendrons, the man on the dune began to take on a different aspect entirely.

Asey grinned, and kept the car on the Shore Road. He was getting old, he decided. Old and soft. He didn't need any barking Colt to cope with that fellow if he happened to run into him. After all, the fellow had jumped and run like a rabbit when Jane screamed the other night at the sail loft.

Near the end of the shore road, a grey sedan passed him going in the opposite direction.

And, as it passed, Asey noticed that it put on a

burst of speed. Simultaneously, he realized that the driver was wearing a dark felt hat with a turned-down brim.

Asey made a U-turn that scraped a stone wall, and started after the grey sedan.

He jammed his foot down on the accelerator, and almost at once reduced the pressure. There were, as Jane had put it, hordes of men with dark felt hats and turned-down brims. It would be foolish of him to race after an innocent tourist and force him to the side of the road. Not just foolish, either, he thought. It would be high-handed, unwarranted, and unwise.

On the other hand, if this happened to be the man he wanted, it would be equally foolish and unwarranted and unwise to let him flit away and evaporate.

Keeping the car just in sight, Asey followed as it swung off on a side road far beyond Cod Point Lane, toward the Pochet swamp.

Watching the fresh tire marks in the dirt ruts, Asey continued on until the ruts gave out entirely and became rough tracks leading to a weathered frame cabin.

The grey sedan was parked outside.

Asey stopped and leaned his elbows on the wheel. Hanging over the front door was a crudely lettered sign, "Stayawhyl." Beneath it was a newer looking addition which said, "Shangri-la."

There was a bathing suit hanging next to a checked dish towel on the clothesline, a milk bottle on the doorstep, some withered marigolds and tomato plants in a tiny garden on one side.

According to the standards of the Lennox place at Cod Point, or Jeff Gage's big Colonial house on the Shore Road, this cabin on the swamp's edge definitely belonged to the ill-housed third.

Still, Asey thought, you could hardly call those red-checked curtains sinister.

He got out of the car, walked over and knocked at the door.

"Come in!"

Asey pressed down the latch with his thumb, and walked in.

At ten o'clock that night, Hanson and Dr. Cummings found him, neatly bound and gagged, on a couch in the cabin's combination kitchen, dining and living room.

The doctor, as he alternately cut and yanked at the adhesive tape bindings, kept up a running stream of conversation.

"For the love of God, haven't you got sense enough at your age— Did that hurt? I suppose you walked right in here, didn't you, and got biffed on the head, and— Hanson, pass me that ether. I'll take this strip off with it. One of Hanson's recruits would know better than to walk into this sort of thing! Look at that bump, Hanson! What did he hit you with, a flat iron?"

Asey worked his jaw experimentally.

"Gun butt," he said.

"And what else? You've got a cut there that's going to need a stitch or two— For the love of God, haven't people got enough to hunt without having to hunt you, too?"

"Found Slocum?" Asey asked.

"Did he hit you?" Hanson demanded. "Was it Slocum who hit you?"

"I don't know who hit me," Asey said.

Cummings stared at him.

"What!"

Asey licked his lips and moved his jaw from side to side.

"The gentleman invited me in, doc, an' in I went."

"Out you went, you mean! Asey, d'you realize you told Jane Lennox that you were going to Slocum's? And that we've combed forty-nine thousand acres for you in the vicinity of Slocum's? Don't try to stand up, you unmitigated idiot! D'you realize that it's simply God's work that we saw your car?"

"Thought someone would," Asey said. "It was the only precaution I took. I dug a little hole with my toe an' dropped the key in an' covered it over, as I got out. Practically the only laugh I had since noon today was listenin' to bozo tryin' to start that car. I think he had some notion of drivin' it into the swamp."

Cummings snorted. "What quaint ideas you have about precautions! Anyway, you owe Hanson a vote of thanks. He got Sam to rig up the wrecker spotlight on his coupé, and he's been on every road between here and Quashnet, playing that light around to find some trace of you."

"Thanks, feller," Asey said. "I'll find you some day—"

"Don't make him blush," Cummings said, "and lean your head over. I think I'll fix this up at the office. Hey, come back with that lantern, Hanson!"

"I was just looking around. The place looks cleared out."

"Bozo picked up his toothbrush an' everything," Asey said. "Seems like he's gone for good."

"I'll have some prints taken," Hanson said, "and we can trace his car— What's the number?"

"Massachusetts mud," Asey said, "for the first

three figures, then two-four, an' then more mud. Grey Ford Tudor, last year's model, an' a strictly routine job. Not even fancy bumper guards."

"Just one of those things," Cummings said, "that you can instantly recognize and put your finger on. Feel okay? Then let's start back. Hanson, what are you writing?"

"Blank, blank, blank," Hanson said, "two, four, blank. We've picked up cars on less'n that. Can you drive him back okay, doc? I want to stay here and look around."

"I'll drive, myself," Asey said. "There's nothin' the matter with me outside of some stiffness. I had a nice rest, after all my Slocum huntin' for the last two nights. Got prints from Slocum's house, Hanson? N'en you can check an' see if this was him, but I don't think it was."

Hanson agreed. "It isn't his car, anyway. His Ford's a black Fordor, and it had a five digit plate. You get along to the doc's, Asey. I'll be over and see you later."

Cummings was unusually silent on the ride back to Wellfleet.

"The only kindly thing," he remarked as Asey turned the car into his driveway, "I can say about this escapade of yours is that it got me out of going to that damned Saturday night bridge at the Tomlinsons'. What my wife sees in the Tomlinsons, I'll never know. And why the hell does that idiot girl of ours turn out every light in the place!"

"Audrey?" Asey asked.

"We've got a new idiot," Cummings said. "She calls herself Marlene, and you should see what she does with telephone messages. Wait till I snap on a light!"

Asey beat the doctor to the hall light by thirty seconds.

"That's to show you that you don't need to coddle me," he said.

"That's simply showing off. Marlene!" Cummings stood at the foot of the stairs in the hall and bellowed. "Marlene! Any calls?"

A wraithlike figure appeared on the upper landing.

"No calls, doctor, but the package came. It was two dollars. I paid the man."

"What package? That serum? Did you put it in the ice box?"

"It's in the waiting room," Marlene said in a crushed voice. "I paid the two dollars—"

Cummings opened the waiting room door and snapped on the light.

For a moment he surveyed the large, brown paper wrapped package that took up most of the room between the center table and the left wall.

Then he looked at Asey.

"Uh—" he said, and gulped. "Will you open that, or—uh—shall I?"

Asey walked to the office beyond, and returned with two pairs of surgical scissors, one of which he passed to the doctor.

Then he knelt down, and cut the heavy manila cord.

Under the third layer of brown paper was a layer of corrugated paper, and under that were several flat, rectangular objects the size of a book, wrapped in newspaper.

"What're those?" Cummings demanded. "Books? Pamphlets?"

"Dry ice."

"What?"

"Dry ice," Asey said. "There's a lot more underneath."

Cummings gulped.

"I'm still praying," he said, "that this *is* a mummy. I'm still praying that this is a mummy, and someone's idea of a joke. I'm going out of this room, and you call me back when you've undone those other brown paper layers. You call me, and tell me it's not a body, it's a mummy, and someone has sent it to me as a joke!"

The doctor went out of the room, but after a restless minute in the hallway, he returned.

He watched as Asey removed the last layer of brown paper and revealed the face of a body.

"My God!" Cummings said. "It isn't Slocum! Who is she? Asey, who *is* she?"

SEVEN

"WHO is the girl? Who—" Cummings was so excited that his voice broke. "Who is this girl? Who *is* she?"

"I don't know," Asey said. "I never saw her before, either!"

"But what—but what—" Cummings swallowed, and started over again. "But why— I mean, how did— Who *is* she?"

"Doc," Asey said, "I don't know what or how or why, or who she is, any more'n you do!"

Cummings walked to the hall in measured, cautious steps, as if he were afraid that the floor might suddenly burst open before him and disclose a vast abyss.

"Mar—"

"Wait, doc," Asey said. "Let's look things over before you get Marlene down here. Doc, look at that paper. Look at that manila cord—"

"I have no desire to look at that brown paper

and that manila cord!" Cummings said. "I have no interest in either! What I want to know is, who *is* that girl? Why was she brought here? How was she brought here? Who brought her? What for? That's what I want to know, and the cord and paper don't interest me that much!" The doctor snapped his fingers.

"They ought to," Asey said. "Look, doc. This is new brown paper that come off a roll. This is new cord. This isn't the sort of stuff that most people have kickin' around the house. Nor is the ice—"

"That's perfectly true, Asey," the doctor said with elaborate sarcasm. "That's an incredibly brilliant bit of deduction. It's true. Practically no household ever has on hand new brown paper or balls of manila cord. Or dry ice. Oh." He paused. "Oho! I see what you mean! It came from a store!"

The doctor sat down suddenly on one of the stiff-backed waiting room chairs.

"Asey, Slocum has a store! And they make their own ice cream, and it's good, and people drive there from all around for it— We go there, ourselves! And Slocum always packs it with dry ice in the bag! He has frozen vegetables, too, and my wife goes over there and gets 'em, because she says with his dry ice, they don't melt before she gets through with the rest of her shopping! Asey, we've got it.

That's the answer. Slocum's store!" He got up and started again for the hallway. "Hey, Mar—"

"Wait up on Marlene, doc. Let's delve into this a little first— Here, help me take off some more of this brown paper."

The girl, they discovered, was short and thin and dark.

"In her twenties, I'd say," Cummings commented. "Maybe twenty-seven. She— What *are* you staring at so? Is there something I don't see?"

"That coat, doc!" Asey said. "Don't you realize? Look at that tweed coat she's got on! Tweed, doc! Rough, hairy, coarse tweed— Don't you remember?"

"My God!" Cummings said. "You don't mean you— Oh, no. You can't believe that this is the body attached to the tweed sleeve that Jane Lennox stumbled over! The one in the sail loft, Thursday! You can't think that!"

"Why not?"

"That was Thursday, man, and this is Saturday —where's she been since?"

"If you ask me," Asey said, "I think she's been in the refrigerator."

"You mean, this girl was killed at the sail loft, Thursday, and the man you chased took the body away in his car and put her in a refrigerator!"

"I never said that. I—"

"But I think you're right." Cummings knelt down on the floor. "I think she has been put in a refrigerator— Help me carry her into the surgery, Asey, and I'll look into this grisly matter. I'll have to look into it sooner or later— You know what, Asey? I'm going to give up this medical examiner business. I'm getting too old for this sort of thing. I— What's so funny?"

"You been sayin' that," Asey said, "for years. Move that paper, doc, an' I'll lift her."

"I'd better fix your head up first," Cummings said. "Come in here, and sit down, and let me sew you up. Asey, I'm speechless. Never in my life have I seen things to equal the goings on of this night!"

"That's the way I felt Thursday— Hey, what are you doing?"

"Just shaving off a bit of your hair. Sit still," Cummings said. "I think this is a judgment on me, Asey. Probably if I'd gone off and played bridge with the Tomlinsons, this would never have happened at all!"

Briskly and efficiently, the doctor sewed up the cut on Asey's head.

"There," he said. "That's that. You look like a college freshman in a dink, but you can always cover up the bandage with your yachting cap if you want. Now, let's see to her!"

Half an hour later, Cummings peeled off his rubber gloves and walked into the waiting room where Asey sat smoking.

"I think you're right, Asey. I think she was killed Thursday, and there's no doubt that the body's been kept in a refrigerated place. Incidentally, Slocum has a large refrigerated room in his store. Place where you keep meats and all. Asey, are you sure that the man at the loft couldn't have been Slocum? Are you sure it wasn't Slocum who put you out of the picture today?"

"I don't know about the fellow today," Asey said. "I never set eyes on him. But I don't think it was Slocum at the loft. I never did think so."

Cummings wanted to know why he was so sure.

"I looked at some of Slocum's campaign pictures yesterday," Asey said, "an' I just been lookin' at one in last week's 'Item' you got here. The fellow I chased Thursday wasn't near so tall or bony. What'd you find out?"

"I didn't go into the matter of clothes and labels," Cummings said. "I left that for Hanson to worry over. There's nothing in her pockets— Ever stop to think about pockets, Asey? A man has so many, you're sure to find something in one of 'em, even if it's just shreds of tobacco from cigarettes. But a woman's pockets never have anything in 'em. She puts all her junk into a bag. And you don't have her bag, you know practically nothing about her. Sure there's no bag in that paper on the floor? Did you look again?"

"Yup. No bag. What'd you find out?"

"Well," Cummings said, "she was hit just about two inches below the place where you got hit. And with considerable more force. Blackjack, I think. The first blow killed her, I think, and the others were added for good measure after she fell. You can read my report tomorrow and get all the details, but that's the gist of the thing."

"What about the ice situation?"

"The body's been kept in a refrigerator, Asey, or in a refrigerated room. The dry ice is something comparatively recent. Someone took the body from where it was, and packed it up with the brown paper and dry ice, and brought it here. And so forth and so on. I can add a lot but nothing that would be of much value to you. For example, I'm sure she was taken by surprise, because there aren't any marks or bruises, or signs of a struggle. And now, I shall summon the anaemic Marlene, and listen to her version of what took place. I warn you, she dissolves into tears at the drop of a hat, and she'll probably have hysterics all over the place."

"Maybe," Asey suggested, "you'd better let me ask her things."

He had a mental vision of Marlene's inevitable collapse if Cummings were allowed free rein.

"Maybe you'd better. But," the doctor added, "be sure you find out all the things I'm still burning to know. Who *is* the girl, who brought her here, and how, and why." He walked toward the hall door, and then hesitated. "Asey, what about knots?"

"What knots?"

"On that manila cord. Sherlock Holmes always looked at knots, and knew that the man who tied 'em was a sailor, or a chimney sweep, or something."

Asey grinned. "Wish I could be as quick on the trigger, doc, but they ain't anything out of the ordinary in the line of knots. I don't think that you or I would make anything any different."

"Sometimes you disappoint me," Cummings said. "Marlene! Hey, Marlene, will you come down here a minute?"

Marlene still looked wraithlike even under the glare of the waiting room chandelier. Clutching her pink wrapper around her thin figure, she looked anxiously at the doctor.

"Did you get the package all right? The man came to the back door first, and by the time I got down, he'd gone to the front door. Then he went around back, and I went to the front, and then—"

"What time did the man bring it?" Asey asked.

"Oh, just a little while before you came. I'd just gone up to bed."

"That would be around ten-thirty or so. I see. Now, did you happen to know the man who brought the package, Marlene?"

"Oh, yes," Marlene said. "It was the expressman. From the truck."

"Uh-huh. But do you know his name?" Asey asked. "Did you ever see him before?"

"Is anything missing?" Marlene inquired unhappily. "I watched him all the time, but I had to leave him alone here while I went upstairs— Don't tell me he took something!"

"This," Cummings explained to Asey, "is because of a little experience we had the other day with a fake drug salesman. He cleaned out my cash box. You don't know the name of the man—is that right? You never saw him before?"

Marlene's underlip began to quiver. She pointed out, defensively, that she had only been in town for ten days.

"There, there!" Asey said. "Don't cry! Tell us what he looked like."

"He had on a hat like expressmen wear," Marlene said. "And like a brown overall, with a zipper. And finally he brought the package in the front door, and I paid him the two dollars."

"There!" Cummings said. "That's what I thought you said when we came in!" He wagged his forefinger at her. "You paid someone two dollars for that package?"

"Shouldn't I ought to have? Shouldn't I of paid? He said there was two dollars due. He said it was C.O.D. So—so I got two dollars, out of my own money, and I paid it. I—I thought you'd pay me right back!"

Marlene dissolved in tears.

"There!" Cummings said. "I told you she would, Asey. You won't get another coherent word out of her for half an hour!"

Asey reached for his wallet, and then turned to the doctor.

"Give me your wallet, doc. That fellow cleaned me out. Marlene— Hey, Marlene. Here!"

"That's a ten!" Cummings protested.

"I know. But if she hadn't anted up, maybe we mightn't have got that package," Asey said. "Think

of that side. Marlene, look. That's right. Take it.
Now, tell us just what the expressman said to you,
an' what you said to the expressman, an' what he
did, an' what you did. Go on, now."

Marlene sniffed. "He said, 'This is a heavy package, sister, where'll I put it?' And I said, 'Put it in
the waiting room.' Then he said, 'Know what this
package feels like, sister? It feels like a body.' And
I said, 'Does it?' And he said, 'Yes, sister, it does.
Is this the room you mean?' And I said, 'Yes.' So
he put it in here. Then I went up and got the two
dollars— Oh. Before that, after he put the package
down in here, he said, 'This is a C.O.D., sister.
There's two bucks due.' Then I got the money, and
then I come down, and I paid him. And then he
said, 'Here's your receipt, sister,' and he wrote his
name on it, and I said, 'Thanks.' And then he
went."

Asey drew a long breath. "Er—you got that receipt, now?"

Marlene nodded.

"I wonder," Asey said, "if you'd let me— Hold
it, doc! If you'd let me see the receipt, please?"

"I'll go get it," Marlene said. "It's up in my
room. It won't take me a minute to get it, mister."

"It," Dr. Cummings was exercising all his self-
control, "it better hadn't!"

He snatched at the receipt when Marlene returned, but she drew it back out of his reach and presented it, with a limpid smile, to Asey.

"Thanks, Marlene," Asey said. "That's all. We'll call you if we want you again."

"Did he take much?" Marlene asked.

"Who? Did who take much?" Cummings retorted.

"The expressman."

"Marlene," Cummings said, "go upstairs! Quick —scoot! Before I forget myself. Asey, what's the name?"

"Craddock," Asey said. " 'Rcd $2, Craddock.' Craddock. Huh. I've heard that name before today—"

"Old Jabe Craddock made that dummy of Slocum, remember?" Cummings said. "But this would be one of the other brothers. Pete's the one in the trucking business. I'll phone him."

"I think," Asey said, "that Brother Craddock deserves a personal visit, doc. I'll seek him out an' go into this matter with him— Whereabouts does he live?"

"Pochet. I'll see." Cummings flipped through the pages of the phone book. "Craddock. Abram, Bert, Carl, Daniel— You must remember the Craddocks, Asey. There used to be seven brothers, and they've all got about seven sons apiece. Here we are. Peter. East Commercial Street, Pochet. I think it's just this side of the Methodist Church. Asey, I don't understand this. Pete's a good, solid citizen! Where'd he ever get hold of that girl's body? And why did he leave it here as a C.O.D.?"

Asey shrugged.

"He must have guessed what it was!" Cummings went on. "You heard that idiot say he said it felt like a body! But it's the C.O.D. part that gets me! Leaving a body here is criminal enough, but making me pay for it is more criminal! I think it's— What's so funny?"

"I was just thinkin' of the headlines," Asey told him. " 'Cape Cod Medico has Criminal C.O.D.' "

"It isn't funny! What'll my wife say when she hears?"

"She'll probably tell you that you'd ought to have played bridge with the Tomlinsons," Asey said. "Well, I'll go see Craddock. You stay here so you can tell Hanson all if he comes or phones. You might even try to get in touch with him."

The Craddock house turned out to be many doors removed from the Pochet Methodist Church, and before he located it, Asey began to feel a vague kinship with Paul Revere. The inhabitants of East

Commercial Street waked easily, but they gave the impression of reaching for a gun.

Pete Craddock, wearing a striped bathrobe over his pyjamas, finally let him in after repeated knockings and bangings.

"Oh, *Asey* Mayo! Sure, I know. Come in. I couldn't hear what you was saying, outside. I know you. Your cousin Syl belongs to my lodge— Nothing the matter with Syl, is there?"

"As far as I know, Syl's in the pink," Asey said. "Look. I come to see you about a package left at Doc Cummings's in Wellfleet tonight. Did you leave one there?"

Pete laughed heartily.

"Gee, yes. Say, what was *in* that? It felt like a body. It was just like a body."

"It was," Asey said.

Pete failed to grasp the significance of Asey's intonation.

"It sure was!" he said. "I told my wife so. Honest, the things the doc gets! Guinea pigs, rats, mice! And the stuff summer patients send him for presents! I delivered a goat to him once."

"Where'd you get that package tonight?" Asey decided to find out as much as he could before enlightening Pete as to the contents.

"Oh, just as I was going to bed, this fellow phoned. He said his driver left it by mistake at the mail boxes by the bluff. So—"

"What fellow?"

"Oh, one of the Boston express fellows," Pete said.

"Which one? What was his name?"

"To tell you the truth, I didn't catch the name," Pete said. "Them names don't mean anything, anyway. They're somebody's express one week, and something else the next. Anyway, he asked would I go to the bluff mail boxes and get this package, and deliver it to Cummings. He said to collect two bucks. Between you and me," Pete added, "I guess this fellow's driver got drunk and messed the deliveries up. This fellow didn't come right out an' say so, but I kind of got that idea. Well, two bucks is two bucks, so I drove over and picked up the package and took it to the doc's. Say, you know what someone sent the doc once last year, as a joke? You know what I delivered?"

"I know," Asey said, "what you delivered tonight. Look, was there a tag on this package?"

"Why, gee, I never thought to look!" Pete said. "This fellow said the package'd be there, and it was, and I just loaded it in. Honest, I never knew anything more like a body than that package. What was it?"

"A body," Asey said. "Thanks a lot."

Craddock was still too dazed when Asey left even to say good bye.

He found Hanson waiting at Dr. Cummings' when he returned. Both men blinked as they heard how Craddock had come into possession of the body.

"You see," Asey said, "it was easy as pie. An' very bright. Somebody did the body up, an' then phoned Craddock an' give him this song an' dance about the driver makin' a mistake. Craddock fell for it. Then the fellow loaded his bundle into his car, an' drove over to the mail boxes by the bluff road, an' unloaded it. It's lonesome enough out there by the bluff this time of year so's there wouldn't be much chance of bein' seen. Then I s'pose he hung around out of sight, so as to make sure that no one but Craddock took his package. An' after Craddock came an' took it, this fellow just upped an' left. I call it," Asey concluded, "pretty smart."

"It's brilliant," Cummings agreed. "As nice a piece of body disposing as I ever heard of. Most people go at it so clumsily, like that Portygee who carved his wife up into all those little pieces. That was before your time, Hanson, but Asey remembers that. The man made such a hideous mess, he had to dump virtually the whole house into the wash tub. And then the neighbors got suspicious, seeing so much washing out, because they weren't a cleanly family. But what about the C.O.D. part, Asey?"

"That," Asey said, "is sheer genius. You got a body, an' you want to get rid of it. But it ain't easy to get rid of a body, an' things is all complicated by this huntin' Henry Slocum. You can't march off to the woods an' bury it, or toss it into the ocean, for fear of bein' spotted by someone huntin' Slocum. See what happened to Jeff and Jane, tryin' to get rid of that dummy!"

"Yes," Cummings said, "but what about this C.O.D.?"

"I'm gettin' to it. You decide it would be nice to present the body you can't get rid of to someone else, an' let them solve the problem for you. Pickin' you was neat, doc."

"I don't see why, Asey! I'm not an undertaker, or a mortician!"

"Nope, but you're medical examiner. There's a nice touch there. But this fellow with the body don't want to bring it here to you himself. He don't want to be seen. He's got to have someone else bring it to you, an' it ain't one of them errands you can even ask your best friend to do for you."

"Why would he have to bring it here anyway?" Hanson inquired. "Seems to me he's making a lot of trouble for himself."

"Looks to me," Asey said, "as if he didn't want the body to be found where it might have been found. Don't ask me why. I s'pose he has his reasons. Anyway, see the problems he had to solve. The logical person to deliver a package is a truckman or an expressman. But this fellow can't take his package to an expressman an' make a deal for deliverin' it without bein' seen. He can't ask an expressman by phone to deliver it without offerin' somethin' in the line of pay. So, the fellow calls the expressman, an' tells him to get the package at a nice remote spot, an' to deliver it to you, an' collect on delivery."

"On the whole," Cummings said, "I don't know which is worse, having a murdered girl delivered to me as a C.O.D. package, or listening to your explanation. Why, for God's sake, why two dollars? Why *two?*"

"It's a nice sum," Asey said. "Makes it worth the expressman's while. As Craddock said, two bucks is two bucks. An' it's also a sum that's likely to be kickin' around a house. Marlene forked over two dollars, but I don't think she'd have forked over ten, or even five. The job was worth any amount to the fellow who was gettin' the body off his hands, but he had to do his figurin' on a basis of what Craddock would be able to collect here with ease. Marlene wouldn't have paid much more than two, an' Craddock probably wouldn't have gone out an' got the package an' delivered it for much less."

"Suppose I'd been here?" Cummings demanded. "That knocks your theory into a cocked hat."

"Why? You'd probably have paid Craddock two bucks," Asey said, "just out of sheer curiosity, wouldn't you? You'd have found out about the body that much sooner, but you wouldn't have found out any more than you know now. An' isn't this Saturday night bridge game a pretty general habit?"

"It is, if my wife can drag me to it." Cummings thought for a moment. "Asey, if Pete Craddock suspected that the package contained a body, why didn't he do something about it?"

"He did. He told his wife it felt like a body."

"Why didn't he call the police?"

"Wa-el," Asey drawled, "he seemed to be pretty accustomed to deliverin' fantastic things to you. He specifically mentioned guinea pigs an' goats."

Cummings nodded slowly. "Yes, I guess you're right. Now I think of it, Craddock was the one who delivered that jar of embryos that broke. I see your point."

"Say," Hanson said, "if this fellow that sent the body knew you, doc, wouldn't he know that you'd be out hunting Asey, too?"

"That's an idea," Cummings said. "Certainly enough people did know that we were hunting Asey. Hm. You might even carry it a step farther, and say that if he knew Asey was lost and out of the way, it was a beautiful time to carry out his C.O.D. notion. By the way, Hanson, d'you suppose Syl's still combing the roads from Quashnet to Weesit, hunting Asey? I hope he and Sam don't get lost. As far as I'm concerned, I've gone on my last man hunt for some time to come."

"You forget," Asey said, "that Henry Slocum is still among the missin'. We also lost a man with a dark felt hat an' turned-down brim, too."

Hanson shook his head wearily.

"I'm tired of hunting Slocum," he said. "I'm sick of the sound of his name. I'm not so tired of the other fellow, because we haven't really hunted him yet. But I phoned, and McGovern's already got someone working on that plate number. He'll have it tomorrow, and then we'll start in on him. There's one thing about this body of this girl. At least we got it. No matter the trouble it means and if we don't know who she is, we got it. Asey, I've been thinking, maybe we've gone at Slocum from the wrong angle. Maybe he hasn't vanished into thin air because of something someone's done to him. Maybe it's because of something he's done, himself."

"Has the doc been tellin' you about the dry ice, an' the brown paper, an' Slocum's store?"

"Well, out of all the places the ice and the paper might have come, we got to start looking somewhere," Hanson said. "We might as well start with his store. There isn't really a lot we can do tonight, but maybe, just for fun, we might look into it."

"Okay," Asey said. "Let's. You coming, doc?"

"Waiting for an ambulance," Cummings said briefly. "I want to get this out of here before my wife gets home. I hope I do!"

Asey chuckled.

"Okay, Hanson. We'll roust out that clerk—what was his name, doc, that wispy man?"

"Smith. For some obscure reason," the doctor yawned, "he's known as Beans. Lives at Mrs. Harkins's boarding house. Just beyond the A and P. I know, because I treated him for a cold."

"I hope it's nearer the A and P," Asey said, "than Craddock's place was to the Methodist Church. Take some samples, Hanson. Any ice left?"

"In the refrigerator," Cummings said. "I'll get a piece if you really want one."

The wispy Mr. Smith was routed, some twenty minutes later, from his bed at Mrs. Harkins's boarding house in Quashnet. Rather unwillingly, he admitted that he had a key to Slocum's store, and he added crossly that they'd have to wait till he got dressed, because he'd have to go along, too.

"I got," he said darkly, "all the responsibility of that store!"

Hanson and Asey waited for him outside in the roadster.

"Had much trouble running the place without Slocum?" Asey inquired when Mr. Smith finally appeared.

"Nobody knows the trouble I had," Smith told him, and lapsed into a gloomy silence.

He let them into the store, turned up the lights, and hung his cap on a hook by the door.

"What was it you wanted?" he asked.

"Brown wrappin' paper," Asey said, "corrugated paper, an' manila cord— Get 'em out, Hanson. Like these."

Smith looked closely at the samples, and then waved his hand in the direction of the near counter.

"Over there. Take all you want. What else?"

"Dry ice. Where's the dry ice department?"

"Dry ice, dry ice!" Smith said. "Sometimes I wish they'd never invented the stuff! All day long people been wanting dry ice! Will I put some dry ice in the ice cream package! Will I put just a dab of dry ice in the frosted peas— Well, we haven't *got* any. We *should* have. They said they left it, like they always do on Saturday. But I haven't seen it. I don't know why— Is that all the cord and paper you wanted?" he added indignantly as Hanson strolled around the counter. "Just those little pieces?"

"Exactly the same, Asey," Hanson said. "Of course, they may not have come from here—"

"Well, they did!" Smith said. "There's nobody else with that kind of cord and paper hereabouts! That's good stout paper, and good stout cord, and you won't find it in any cheap store. We don't wrap our merchandise in cheap, flimsy paper, or stuff a lot of cans into thin paper bags. We only got quality!"

"You're sure," Hanson said, "that these pieces of paper and cord we brought with us came from this store?"

"Of course they did! I could have told you so at home," Smith said, "if you'd just shown 'em to me there. You didn't need to get me out of bed and drag me over here to learn that!"

"An' today's lot of dry ice didn't come," Asey

said. "Well, well. Had a lot of customers today, too, huh?"

"I told you, nobody knows the day I put in!" Smith said. "Look, don't you *want* anything? Don't you want to *buy* anything? What do you want, anyway?"

"I want to know about today," Asey said. "And believe me, Mr. Smith, when I say it's important enough to have got you out of bed. You had a lot of customers— Did you have many strangers?"

Smith looked at him.

"Look here," he said, "I got to this store at seven o'clock this morning, and I went to work on the orders. At eight, Harry Evans—he comes in on Saturdays—he called up and said he was sick, and couldn't come. And his son that works here Saturdays, too, he had a chance to go to Boston with the Scouts, so he'd gone. Do you understand what that means? It means I was here alone in this store, all day Saturday—a Saturday, mind you! From seven till half past ten tonight! That's what it means. And you ask me if I had a lot of strange customers!"

"We wanted to know," Hanson began, "if—"

"Well, you know now! And then shipments started coming in. And the kid that drives the order truck has a flat. And the orders are late, and people start phoning. You go out into that back store room, and you look at the packing cases that came just from Jordan and Phillips! I haven't even checked the invoices. I don't know where they are— I haven't counted the cash. I didn't touch the books—"

"I'm willin' to believe," Asey said, "that we better take you back to bed before you cave in. The sum an' substance of what happened today is that you didn't notice who came in here, or what they did."

"That," Smith said, "is it."

"It's clear enough, Asey," Hanson said. "In all the mess and everything, anyone could take paper and cord. Where do you keep extra paper, out back in that store room? And there's back doors, too, aren't there? It's a cinch, Asey. The ice was left, and he took that too. It wouldn't have been any job at all to take those things."

"A hiking club," Smith said suddenly.

"Huh?"

"You asked about strangers, didn't you? Well, there was a hiking club. Eight pounds of top, ground. We didn't have it, so I gave 'em bottom. They didn't know the difference. Then there was tourists. Must have been a lot. We ran out of frankforts. Then—"

"Don't think any more," Asey said. "You told

us what we wanted to know, that most anyone at all could have come here most any time today, an' got paper an' string an' a supply of dry ice. An' of course Slocum's got keys to the store, hasn't he?"

"Slocum!" Smith said bitterly. "Don't say Slocum to me! When Hank sobers up from this one, I'm quitting— I don't care if I don't get another job this winter, I'm quitting!"

"Think he's off on a bat, do you?" Asey inquired.

"He always has been before, when he went away like this. I never did believe that sick friend story. I know Slocum. Of course when people ask me about him, I say he's still with his sick friend. It wouldn't be good for trade to say anything else."

"You don't think that Slocum's the victim of any foul play, huh?" Asey asked.

Smith sniffed. "I heard the Collins boys and some of the others talking about a plot! Plot, nothing. I tell you, I know Slocum. Of course," he added, "I thought he'd cut this kind of thing out. I know he promised Irma to cut it out. I thought for a while this summer that Irma'd reformed him. I guess she thought so, too. But the minute she goes away, he's off again. I told Collins that. I told him when the cat was away, the mice 'ud play."

"Come on, Asey." Hanson was restless. "I want to get back and get started!"

"Wait a sec," Asey said. "Wait a sec. Tell me, Smith. Is Irma short, an' thin, an' dark haired?" He described the girl whose body was at Cummings'. "Would that by any chance be Irma?"

"Sounds like her," Smith said. "There's a picture of her on his desk in the office— Want to see it?"

Asey and Hanson were at his heels as Smith crossed the store and led the way to the little office.

Hanson took one look at the picture in the gilt frame, and then he pulled out his notebook.

"Full name?"

"John Henry— Oh, Irma's? Irma Dine. I don't know her middle name."

"And she's Slocum's girl? Was Slocum engaged to her?"

"Well—" Smith seemed a little confused by Hanson's sudden and intense interest in Irma—"well, I used to think so. But now I don't know. Lately he seems to be with that Mrs. Lennox all the time."

"I see," Hanson said. "Irma lives here in Quashnet, does she? When'd you see her last?"

"Why, she went to Boston— Let's see, I guess it was on Tuesday she drove to Boston. She's gone on her vacation," Smith said. "I thought it was sort of funny she would go away this week, with the school dedication and the big rally and everything. You'd think that where she and Slocum was so thick, she'd stay around and hear his speech—"

He broke off as a car horn started to blare insistently outside the store.

"Sounds like your horn, Asey," Hanson commented.

"You know what that is?" Smith said irritably. "It's somebody sitting out in their car blowing their horn for me to come out and sell 'em a quart of ice cream. It always happens if there's lights on here at night. Somebody sees the light, and stops and starts blowing the horn for ice cream— Well, you go out and send 'em away! Because I'm not going to wrap up another package today. I won't even get anybody a loaf of bread. Not even a slice!"

Asey grinned and went to the door. Jane Lennox was standing outside.

"Oh, Asey!" she said as he let her in. "Asey, I'm all but dead. I'm a wreck. Mother, and Dad, and Ty, and William, and Uncle Jeff, and Garfield —we've all been hunting you since afternoon! They've just gone on home, but I drove around by the doctor's, and he said I'd probably find you here. Asey, was it our man that got you? The dark felt hat one?"

"I didn't see him," Asey said, "but I have this

horrid suspicion that it was. Did—er, did the doc tell you—?"

Jane nodded.

"I saw her. They were taking her out when I got there. Poor Irma— Asey, isn't it ghastly! I feel terrible!"

"You knew her?"

"Knew her? Of course! She's Dad's secretary. She lived with us."

EIGHT

ASEY was awakened Sunday forenoon by the sounds of a violent battle of words between his cousin Jennie and her husband Syl.

It was the routine Sunday morning battle, and it always took place, rain or shine, at the side door. On other days, Syl and Jennie largely confined their bickerings to the kitchen and the shed, but on Sundays they moved out to the side door directly under Asey's open bedroom windows, and then they opened their mouths and raised their voices and let themselves go. Asey sometimes wondered if perhaps it wasn't Jennie's backhand method of including him in her customary reproachful command to Syl.

"Syl, you get to church!"

"Now, Jennie, I don't see how you can expect me to go to church today. I got—"

"Syl, change your clothes, an' get to church!"

The order was accompanied by a swishing noise,

and a patter of footsteps retreating down the side walk.

Without even bothering to close his eyes, Asey could conjure up the picture of Jennie, armed with a broom, towering menacingly over her short husband.

"I got to see Asey." Syl was coming back up the path. "You put down that broom, now. I got things to tell him. I got things I been trying to tell him since yesterday noon. If somebody in the family's got to go to church, you go yourself! I'll stay here." Syl paused for breath. "Well, why *don't* you go?"

"It just so happens," Jennie said with dignity, "I got things to tell him myself! I guess if what you got to say's waited this long, it can wait a paltry few minutes longer while you go to church!"

"I ain't goin'."

"You are!"

There was a great deal more of the same, and Asey sighed as he listened to it.

He would have liked to yell out and tell them that they were disturbing him, that he wanted a chance to be quiet, and collect his thoughts. But if he made any move to silence them, Jennie would burst into tears, and Syl would go around all day with a hurt, distressed look on his face.

Asey sighed again, and got out of bed. He knew that his cousins' interest in him and his affairs was prompted only by their devotion to him. He appreciated that, and all that Jennie and Syl did for him. But sometimes he found them a little overpowering.

They were still going strong when Asey finished dressing, and they showed no signs of weariness nor any indication of running down when he strolled into the dining room.

"Mornin'," he said. "Havin' a nice workout?"

"Asey, I'm glad to see you!" Syl said. "You'll never know what a night Sam an' I put in. We hunted every inch of ground between Quashnet and Weesit an' back again for you, an' I never was any gladder'n when I heard that Hanson'd found you— Hanson come here early this mornin', but Jennie said you'd give orders you wasn't to be disturbed. *I* wanted to call you, but she had her way!"

"It wasn't anything to wake you up for," Jennie said. "I asked him. He just wanted to tell you that the cabin by the swamp where he found you belonged to an Orleans man that rents it. His regular renters left last week, an' he rented it again Friday to a feller in a dark suit an' a dark felt hat an' a grey car. Feller said he was goin' to do some fishin', an' his name was—"

"Jones, or Black, or White or Green?" Asey inquired.

"No. Brown. That's all the Orleans feller knows

about him. Hanson said they was still goin' after them muddy number plates, an' they still hadn't found a single trace of Henry Slocum anywheres. An' it wasn't worth wakin' you to tell you that, I thought— Syl, what are you pawing Asey for?"

"I ain't! I just wanted to see how his cut was, Jennie!" Syl protested.

"If it wasn't all right, he'd say so. Asey, did Syl wake you up, hollerin'? I was tryin' to give you a chance to get some rest this mornin', but he had to come along an' holler, holler, holler!"

"You hollered," Syl said. "I didn't. Asey, I got so much to tell you. You got to come right over to Slocum's—"

"Let the man eat his breakfast!" Jennie said. "Goodness gracious, let him have a meal in peace, can't you? The man hasn't had a peaceful meal since Thursday when his new car come. An' take your hand away from them biscuits! Asey, tell me about that Dine girl. Who d'you think killed her?"

"Don't know, Jennie."

"Where d'you think she was killed?"

Asey shrugged. "Haven't any idea."

"Did you find out *any*thing about her last night?"

"Only that she was Slocum's girl friend, an' Charles Lennox's secretary," Asey said.

"Well," Jennie said, "I know a lot more than

that! It just so happens, Asey, that I heard quite a few things about Irma Dine, an' I think you ought to know 'em!"

"Twenty-two line buzzin' like a hive of bees, hey?"

Jennie bristled as she always did when Asey made any comment about the twenty-two line, and said she was sure she didn't see how anyone could ever expect to hear anything, if anyone didn't listen once in a while to what people were saying.

"I kind of thought," Asey said gently, "that you'd do some listenin', Jennie, an' that's why I declined Hanson's invitation to do any more investigatin' with him last night. I told him you'd have all the dope there was all ready for me today. Let's hear it."

"Well, Irma Dine's lived with the Lennoxes ever since they come down in June from Boston. He needed a secretary because he was writin' a book— I didn't know he wrote, Asey. I thought he worked in a bank."

"He owned it," Asey said, "an' now he's retired an' writin' the history of Quashnet."

"Of Quashnet? For heaven's sakes, what *for?*" Jennie said. "That one horse place! Why, I told Syl yesterday, I'd heard more about Quashnet in the last two days than I'd heard in thirty years. I don't know why, but I don't even seem to know much of anyone over there. Well, Asey, this Irma Dine stayed with the Lennoxes. She had a little room in the ell where that couple of theirs live, an' I guess," Jennie said meaningly, "that while Mrs. Lennox ran around with Henry Slocum, I guess Charles Lennox ran around with this girl! There. What do you think of that?"

"Not much," Asey said tranquilly. "Mrs. Lennox went around with Slocum because she was helpin' his campaign—"

"Stuff an' nonsense! You couldn't make me think that's all there was to that, not in a million years!"

"I shan't try, Jennie. But I'd say if Irma Dine was with Charles Lennox to any extent, it was because she was helpin' him with his book. Charles Lennox," Asey said, "don't seem to me the sort of man who'd carry on with a secretary, somehow."

"Well, he took her to the movies all the time! He took her to see every one of the Hardy family pictures that came to the Bijou this summer. And do you know what? He lent her French books!"

"The way you say that," Asey observed, "it sounds like Charles Lennox spent the summer crammin' lewd books down the girl's throat. Jennie, if Lennox lent her French books, I feel awful sure it was a legitimate lendin' of virtuous books."

"She claimed he was teaching her French," Jennie said, "but what'd she want to learn that for, anyway? I don't care what you say, I think it's queer for a man writin' a book about Quashnet to take time off an' teach his secretary French! And they drove around everywheres together in that beach-wagon, to all sorts of back roads an' out of the way places."

"Probably," Asey said, "gettin' material for the history of Quashnet. Jennie, ain't you got anything good to offer in the line of information about this girl?"

"Why, I've told you the good parts— Don't you see, Asey? If Henry Slocum found out that his girl was carryin' on with Lennox, there's a motive for his killin' her!"

"Wouldn't it be more sensible," Asey said, "to kill Lennox?"

"Then," Jennie ignored his question, "if Mrs. Lennox found out about her husband's carryin' on with Irma Dine, she'd have a motive for killin' the girl. An' then, s'pose the girl begun to make demands on Lennox. S'pose she threatened to tell his wife, or wanted him to get a divorce— Then that gives Lennox a motive for gettin' rid of the girl. *I* think," Jennie concluded, "that one's the best."

"Uh-huh," Asey said. "Now, tell me facts. Who is the girl? Has she folks? I don't seem to connect the name of Dine with anything or anyone."

"About fifteen years ago, this Mrs. Dine came to Quashnet, Asey, an' was housekeeper for Martin Snow. An' she married him a year or so later. This is the daughter she brought with her."

Again, by a trick of inflection, Jennie made it sound as if the girl were just something that Mrs. Dine had picked up en route.

"I guess," Jennie went on, "the girl was bright enough. She was valedictorian of her class, an' she worked at Slocum's store, an' roundabouts in Quashnet, an' scraped up enough money to go to business school in Boston. She got through last winter, an' this job for Charles Lennox is her first real one. Now, the way *I* heard it, she asked Lennox for a vacation last week, an' Lennox give her one, an' she went to Boston Tuesday in her car—"

"What kind?" Asey asked.

"Why, I don't know! She was going to stay ten days. Seemed awful funny to me that she'd pick the week of the school dedication an' all to go away for a vacation. Carrie an' I decided she probably flounced off to spite Slocum an' make him mad, an' didn't even tell him where she'd be. I suppose she was jealous of Mrs. Lennox— Of course, as Carrie said, Slocum most likely told the girl that Mrs. Lennox was just helping him in his campaign, and if the girl really loved him, she'd most likely believe him. But she'd be jealous just the same. So she flounced off."

"Where'd she stay in Boston?"

"Nobody seems to know that," Jennie said.

"Wouldn't her mother and step-father know?"

"Good gracious, Asey," Jennie said, "Martin Snow an' Mrs. Dine died ten years ago. The girl hasn't any folks now. She boarded with Snow's sister, Abby Hallet, until she went over to the Lennoxes'. And Abby Hallet didn't know. She told Carrie's cousin so over the phone this mornin'. She said Irma told her she was goin' to hunt up some friend she went to business school with, an' stay with her, an' she'd send a card an' tell her where. But she never sent any card. Mrs. Hallet didn't know a thing. You know who Abby Hallet is, Asey. The flower one."

"The which?"

"Oh, she's the one that always beats Carrie for the best flower prize at the Grange Fair. Asey, Carrie's cousin heard someone say that even the Lennoxes didn't know where Irma Dine was goin' in Boston. Seems awful strange to me that they wouldn't ask her where she was stayin', don't you think?"

"Not awfully." Asey finished his coffee.

"Ain't they got any curiosity at *all?*"

"Not that kind. Are those all the facts you can muster, Jennie? Because if they are, I'm goin' to let you do some more delvin' while I go over to Slocum's with Syl. You hop over to your house an' glue your ear to the phone, an' find out stuff like what kind of a car the girl owned, an' why she took her vacation now, an' where she stayed in Boston, an' how she got back to Quashnet, an' why. Stuff like that."

Jennie thought for a moment.

"Don't you s'pose," she said, "that the girl come back to hear Slocum's speech at the school dedication? Most likely she'd told him she was goin' to stay away from it, an' she didn't want to hear it, but you know how women are. Probably she drove all the way down from Boston just for that—"

"Then where's her car now, if she come in it?" Syl inquired suddenly.

"What's it matter where her car is?" Jennie retorted. "Here's a girl murdered an' carted around like a common bundle, an' after listenin' like a bump on a log for fifteen minutes, all you can think to ask about is where's her car!"

"Well, if she come to Quashnet in her car," Syl said, "she certainly didn't drive away again afterwards, did she? An' with all this huntin' around for

Slocum an' for Asey, I should think a deserted car'd come to light. I should think someone'd have happened on it, somewhere. I should think—"

"*I* should think that somebody else drove her down, an' then drove away again," Jennie said. "That's what I should think. Wouldn't you, Asey?"

Asey shook his head. "The chances are that she was killed by someone down here, Jennie, an' somebody who's still here."

"Why?" Jennie demanded. "Who, down here? Why couldn't she have been killed in Boston, for all you know?"

"Wa-el," Asey said, "the fellow who engineered that business of her body bein' delivered to the doc's last night must have been here on the Cape. Hanson an' I stopped at the Pochet phone office after we took Smith home from Slocum's store, an' though the girl couldn't tell us anything about that call to Craddock, she knew it wasn't any long distance call. It was a local call. I don't mean this fellow has to be a native, Jennie—"

"You said someone down here on the Cape!"

"That's what I meant. The fellow's got to know enough about the place to get that cord an' paper at Slocum's store, an' to leave the body at a deserted sort of place like the bluff mail boxes, an' to pick an expressman like Craddock, someone sort of hearty an' dumb. The fellow don't have to be a native. He can be a summer visitor, or a tourist. But he isn't any stranger on his first trip to the Cape. An' if he is here on the Cape, it'd be hard to drive the girl's car away— I'm glad you brought this up, Syl. It's somethin' I hadn't thought a lot about."

Jennie sniffed.

"I still don't see as it matters if she drove down in her car, or somebody drove her, or she drove in someone else's, or how she came. I don't see it makes much difference. It don't seem to me to matter half as much as Charles Lennox lendin' her French books an' takin' her to the movies night after night. An' anyway, I don't see how you could ever find out."

"I think," Asey said, "that just for fun we'll put the problem up to Hanson. He can get her car plate numbers, an' see if the car's still in Boston, parked in a garage or somewheres. That's the sort of job he loves to tackle."

Syl agreed. "It certainly don't seem that there's anything he likes any better than trackin' down license plates. Why, before he set out to hunt you yesterday, he rushed around an' got your numbers, even! Asey, let's get on to Slocum's. I got an awful lot to show you an' tell you about things over there

at his place. I been wantin' to tell you since yesterday—"

He started pouring out details, but Asey stopped
him.

"Wait'll we get there, will you, Syl? I want to
think."

Although Syl never once opened his mouth as
they drove along toward Quashnet, Asey neverthe-
less found it difficult to engage in any constructive
thinking with Syl's beady eyes focused unwaver-
ingly on his face.

"Syl," he said at last, "I wonder if you'd turn
around an' watch behind us, an' see if there's anyone followin', will you? Keep on lookin' till I tell
you to stop."

But even without the handicap of Syl's discon-
certing stare, Asey had to admit to himself that he
couldn't make much of a beginning at sorting things
out in his mind.

Without doubt it had been Irma Dine's body
which Jane had stumbled over in the sail loft on
Thursday night.

Jane had confirmed that, in a torrent of excited
words, at Slocum's store the night before.

"It was her coat that I felt, Asey. That was the
tweed arm. Hers. I recognized the tweed just now
at the doctor's when I saw them taking her out. I—

I felt it again, to make sure. I knew that Irma had a coat like that. I've seen her wearing it, often. But I wasn't thinking about her Thursday night. I was thinking about Henry Slocum. Maybe I ought to have sensed that it was a woman's arm and not a man's. But—but I'd never stumbled over an arm like that before! I guess I was too frightened to sense anything. And I know I never thought of Irma at all! She never entered my head! Why, she was in Boston, Asey, miles away! She was on her vacation! I never thought of her. But now I know it was Irma."

So much for that, Asey thought.

But had Irma Dine been killed at the loft? And where had her body been kept? It was all right for Hanson and Dr. Cummings to speak airily of refrigerators and refrigerated rooms like that at Slocum's store. But when you came right down to it, very few refrigerators would be large enough to hold the girl's body, even though she was small and thin. And that clerk, Smith, had been in and out of that refrigerated room at the store a million times, by his own account, just on Saturday. It was possible that the body might have been hidden away in such a fashion that Smith wouldn't have noticed it, but Asey doubted that very strongly.

And if the girl had actually been killed at the

loft, how had the body been taken away so quickly after Jane dashed out of the loft? The simplest and probably the best explanation to that was Jane's own figuring the other night: that the felt hatted man whom he had chased was in the loft when Jane herself came there, that he'd hurriedly taken the body to his car on the old lane. Then why, Asey wondered, had the man come back? If he already had the body in the car, ready to drive it away, why had he returned? Would he have taken the chance of leaving the body there in the car while he came back and stood in a pine grove and threw stones for the dog Nosey?

Jane had contended that the man came back for the red wig and the tiny pocket flask.

There, Asey thought, were more headaches, that wig and that flask.

The flask belonged to Slocum, in spite of its bearing Emmet Lennox's initials. Mrs. Lennox had corroborated that Thursday night, after Slocum slatted out of the Lennox house. So you could assume, Asey thought, that if anyone had left the flask in the sail loft on Thursday, Slocum left it.

But the flask had been empty. And not just empty, but washed out. And it seemed silly to think that Slocum would be carrying around an empty flask with him, that night or any other night.

Of course, the girl Irma Dine might have had the flask with her. But Smith said the girl had tried to stop Slocum's drinking. It didn't seem likely that she, under the circumstances, would carry a flask.

"Syl," Asey said suddenly, "why in thunder would you carry with you an empty flask belongin' to someone else, when the chances are that you don't drink, yourself?"

He asked the question largely out of exasperation, and with little expectation of eliciting from Syl anything more than a bewildered "I dunno."

But Syl answered promptly.

"Well, Asey, I guess I might be takin' it to have it fixed for somebody. Maybe it—"

Asey stopped the car and looked at his cousin in admiration.

"Syl, you're right! That's it! Mrs. Lennox said how easy the cap unscrewed! She said it never unscrewed like that before. That's the answer. The Dine girl took the flask to Boston to have it fixed for Slocum. That's why it was empty, an' clean— You know what I bet, Syl? I bet she told him that when he wanted a drink, to confine himself to that little flask, an' he'd never get into trouble. It just held a gill. Yes, Syl, I think you got it. An' the girl had the flask in her coat pocket, an' it slipped out— Let's see, I don't think it could have slipped out

when she fell from that blow. The doc said it was a
hard blow, an' she probably crumpled right up.
I guess it must have slipped out when she was bein'
carried out. The flask's leather covered, an' it's dollars to doughnuts the fellow never heard it drop.
Or maybe he heard it, an' didn't dare take the time
to find it then— Cousin, how did you hit on that?"

"Well," Syl said, "I got Jennie's readin' glasses in
my pocket, but I don't use glasses myself. I had 'em
for a week," he added sheepishly. "She thinks
they're bein' fixed. Anyway, it's the same thing,
Asey. I'm carryin' somethin' for somebody else that
I don't never use myself."

"Haven't got a red wig on you, have you?" Asey
asked.

"Huh?"

"You solved the flask," Asey said, "I thought you
might clear up the wig. Tell me, why would you
wear a red wig?"

Syl looked at him suspiciously. "Is it a joke, like
that one about the black horses eating more than
the white horses? Or to keep your head warm or
something?"

"Nope, I ain't kiddin', Syl. I just want to know,
why would you wear a red wig?"

"Well," Syl said, "I don't know's I would. If I
was bald, I'd wear a black wig, I s'pose, same as my

hair. But on the other hand, even if I was bald, I don't think I'd take to wearin' any wig, anyway. I think I'd just rather be bald."

Asey chuckled. "I think I would, too. But can you think of any reason why you'd wear a red wig, Syl? Any reason at all?"

"Maybe if I was in a play," Syl said. "I might have to be somebody with red hair. Or maybe I might want to look like someone with red hair, anyway, without a play."

"Go on," Asey said encouragingly, "I got that far, myself. Go on, Syl."

"Land's sakes, Asey, what a thing to ask anyone! I can't think of any more reasons why I'd go traipsin' around in a red wig! I don't even know anybody with red hair, except that girl you pay the electric bills to over at the electric office, an' she's more auburn than red! Do *you* know anybody with red hair?"

"Offhand, no," Asey told him, "an' it'd be an awful lot simpler if I did. Well, keep thinkin' about the red wig, Syl, an' let me know if you figger anything out."

"Do you think she was killed right there in the sail loft, Asey?"

Asey shook his head.

"I wish I could be surer of that, Syl. She was dead

when Jane stumbled over her, an' we can guess that the flask slipped out of her pocket when she was carried out. But on the other hand, Jane didn't hear any strange noises when she walked down there. You can't tell how long the body might have been there. Or she might have been killed somewheres else, an' brought there."

"Why?" Syl asked.

"Wa-el," Asey started the car up again, "if you didn't happen to like the Lennox family much, you could cause 'em quite a lot of anguish by leavin' the dead body of Charles Lennox's secretary in the Lennox sail loft. But if someone meant to drag the Lennoxes in, I don't see why they went an' whisked the body right away again. I'd give a lot, Syl, to be able to figure out how the girl got there, an' if she was alive when she come."

"Hanson thinks she was killed there," Syl said. "An' I didn't like to mention this in front of Jennie, with her all riled up about Charles Lennox an' the girl, but I think Hanson's doped it out that Charles Lennox was alone in the house at Cod Point there, all Thursday evenin'. Did you know that?"

Asey nodded.

"Well, Hanson thinks that Jane Lennox an' her father was in cahoots—"

"What?"

"Well," Syl said, "Hanson told me so. He said he'd thought about the mother, but she was over at the school dedication, right up on the platform next to the Governor. So—"

"Can't Hanson do anything but pick on the Lennoxes?" Asey said. "First it was Jeff Gage, an' now Jane an' her father! I thought he was broodin' about Henry Slocum killin' her, last night!"

"I guess he did have that notion, but then Hanson thought it over, an' he figgered that after all, Slocum turned up after the body was found. At least, he turned up Thursday night, an' Jane fell over the body Thursday evenin'. Hanson says if Slocum was goin' to run away, he'd have gone right off the bat, on Thursday evenin'. He— Say, Asey, you're makin' the wrong turn for Slocum's! Asey, ain't you goin' to Slocum's?"

"Nope."

"Well, there ain't any sense in goin' after that grey car, now, Asey! It's gone!"

"Grey car? *What* grey car?"

"Why, that grey Ford sedan that was followin' us!" Syl said impatiently. "You told me to watch, an' I watched. But I guess the feller must have caught on that I was watchin', because he turned off— Why, I asked you if you didn't want to turn round an' go after him, but you just shook your head, an' muttered!"

Asey sighed.

Probably he had shaken his head. Very likely he had shaken his head. But if Syl had said anything about a grey car, it hadn't penetrated his meandering thoughts about the girl and the sail loft and all the rest.

"Where you goin' now?" Syl wanted to know.

"I'm headin' for the Lennoxes' sail loft. An' if you see any more grey cars trailin' us, please let me know!"

Syl looked hurt.

"Why, you sound like I hadn't told you about this one! An' I did. An' besides, I thought you knew all about it anyways— Asey, what do you want to go to the sail loft for, now? Why can't you get along to Henry Slocum's, an' let me show you an' tell you all these things I been tryin' to show you an' tell you for about fifty million years?"

"I'm goin' to the loft," Asey told him, "to see if I can't find somethin' to prove whether the Dine girl was really killed right there, or not. An' I don't know which is goin' to be more confusin', to find that she was, or to find that she wasn't."

"Didn't you look around that place on Thursday?"

"Uh-huh. But all I had was a flash to look around with. Now just you sit tight, Syl. There's plenty of time to go through Henry Slocum's place. An' before Hanson gets any fixed ideas about the Lennox family, I want to do some spade work. See?"

"Seems to me you're goin' to a lot of pains for the Lennox family," Syl remarked, "considerin' as how you never knew any of 'em before Thursday. I can see where you'd want to set Hanson straight about Jeff Gage. You've known him a long while. But you don't know these Lennoxes."

"They're nice, pleasant folks," Asey said, "an' there's no sense in lettin' 'em in for all the unpleasantness they'll get if Hanson decides that Jane an' her father are responsible for that girl's bein' killed. They're no more responsible for it than you are. I know. I was with 'em that evenin'. If they're murderers, Syl, I'm Mickey Mouse!"

Syl cleared his throat elaborately.

"Well, Asey, maybe they are nice folks. But I still claim you don't know a lot about 'em. Now from what I heard, this Jane Lennox's sort of harum-scarum, runnin' around in that Porter ninety miles an hour with that Bricker boy—"

"Drivin' a Porter at high speeds," Asey said, "ain't depraved."

Syl looked at the speedometer. "Well, take Mrs.

Lennox. Maybe she's just interested in Slocum's campaign, like you say, an' not Slocum. But— Well, you wouldn't find Jennie marchin' around helpin' run the campaign of a young fellow like him. You wouldn't find the doc's wife doin' it. Now mind you, I ain't sayin' she's done anythin' wrong, this Mrs. Lennox, but she's put herself in a place where people can raise their eyebrows at her. If she was my wife, I wouldn't like it. An' honest, Asey, don't it seem queer to you that a man in his right mind would retire from bein' a bank president to write the history of Quashnet? I mean—"

"Uh-huh. I get it, Syl. You mean you don't think the Lennoxes is nice folks."

"No," Syl said stubbornly, "I just say, you don't know a lot about 'em! For all you know, Hanson may be right. For—"

Asey put on such a burst of speed that the rest of Syl's sentence was drowned out.

A few seconds later, he drew the roadster up by the rear of the sail loft, and turned to Syl.

"Tell you what, Syl. We'll just look around, an' see if— Wow!"

He and Syl stared in mute fascination at what had been, before the shot rang out, a rear view mirror.

NINE

~~~~~~

SYL was the first to break the silence.

"My," he said in wondering tones, "didn't that bullet whine!"

Asey surveyed the sliver of broken glass on the seat beside him, and the slivers of broken glass on the floor of the car. Then he looked thoughtfully at his imperturbable cousin.

"It was as fine a whine as I ever heard, Sylvanus. If you'd heard it a little mite clearer an' louder, I'd be takin' you home in a basket."

"Oh, I don't think anyone was aimin' at *me,*" Syl said. "They was aimin' at you, Asey. I can't think of anyone hereabouts who'd be wanting to shoot me. 'Course," he added, "I can't think of a soul hereabouts who'd be wanting to shoot you either, can you? I mean, the Lennoxes bein' such nice folks, an' all."

"Syl," Asey said, "I never suspected irony like that from you!"

"Why, that ain't irony, Asey! I can't think of anyone here who'd want to kill you. But I do think someone was aimin' at you an' not me. It just happened that the bullet went between us."

Asey drew a long breath.

"Uh-huh. I guess that's the best way of summin' it up. It just happened to go between us. Syl, do you think it'd be nicer to get up an' walk around an' investigate an' get potted at again, or would you just sit here?"

"Why," Syl said after a moment's consideration, "if they didn't shoot again right off, Asey, I don't think they *will* shoot again, do you? I'd say— Why, there's a dog! Here, feller!"

Nosey bounded up to within a few feet of the roadster, and then circled suspiciously around it, sniffing.

"An' when you get through sniffin'," Asey said, "I'm going to get out an' circle around you suspicious-like, Nosey. Because I got this feelin'—"

"Somebody's comin', Asey!" Syl said. "Listen— isn't that someone whistlin' to the dog? Yes, sir! Yes-sirree. Somebody's comin' through the pine grove yonder— Look, Asey!"

Asey leaned back against the roadster's leather cushions.

"Look, Asey!" Syl said. "Look!"

"I almost don't want to," Asey told him. "Because I keep havin' this feelin' that— Uh-huh. I knew it. I thought so!"

Jane and Charles Lennox appeared, sauntering through the pines.

"Look!" Syl urged. "Look, Asey!"

Charles Lennox was casually twirling a pistol by the trigger guard.

"Asey!" Jane called out. "Hello, Asey!"

"Hulloa, Asey!" Charles waved the pistol. "How are you?"

Asey waited till they reached the car before he answered their jaunty greetings.

"Hunting?" he inquired.

"What? Oh, no," Charles said. "This is a thing of Emmet's that I dug up in the attic just now. I think he used to hunt skunks with it, but we're not after game. We're just menacing."

"You do it," Asey said, "very well. Very well indeed, Mister Lennox!"

Charles was obviously taken aback by the frigid purr in Asey's voice.

"What—er—what d'you mean?" he asked.

Asey pointed to the remains of the rear view mirror.

"Why," he inquired, "do you menace me?"

"Good God!" Charles said. "Did I do that when

I shot this thing off? Oh, I couldn't have, Asey! I couldn't have hit that— Jane, was I aiming this way when I shot?"

"Well, not specifically," Jane said. "But sort of in this direction— Asey, this is awful! We didn't have any idea you were here! I mean, it's an accident! Dad, stop making those noises in your throat, and explain to him that it's an accident!"

"My dear, he knows it is!" Charles said. "I'm so ashamed of myself, I can't think of anything to say, Asey. I've never felt a bigger fool!"

"Who was you intendin' to menace?" Asey asked.

"That infernal man in the dark felt hat!" Charles said. "He came around and scared Mary to death last night— She was alone at the house. The rest of us were out hunting for you, you know. Mary locked herself up in my study, and barricaded the windows. She was in such a state of nerves that she wouldn't unlock the door till William sang a song to prove who he was— Asey, who *is* this man, do you know? What's he lurking around here for? What does he want?"

Asey shook his head.

"Has the feller been here today?" he asked.

"Yes, I caught a glimpse of him snooping around about an hour ago. I yelled at him—that is, I yelled in his general direction, and told him that if he wanted anything, would he please come to the door like a gentleman, and ask for it. I also told him to stop trampling the rhododendrons, and if I caught him slinking around any more, I'd shoot him. So—"

"So then we went to the attic," Jane said, "and dug up this pistol, and found some bullets to fit it, and then we set out to be menacing. That's how this happened, Asey. We were menacing that man. We never intended to menace you!"

"You mean, you was just saunterin' around, firin' hither an' yon sort of aimless, like?" Asey demanded.

"Well," Charles said, "it boils down to that, although as a matter of fact, we only shot once. You see, we thought that perhaps a bit of gunfire would convince this man that I meant what I said. Jane, this is simply horrible to tell him about, isn't it? How in the world can I explain that ten minutes ago, you and I were dancing around, brandishing this gun, and talking about exorcising evil spirits!"

"The horrible part," Jane said, "is that it's the second time, Dad! It's the second time one of us has nearly killed him!"

Asey avoided Syl's eyes.

"Dad," Jane went on, "what can we *do?*"

Charles rubbed his chin reflectively.

"I've been thinking, myself. We can hardly ask

Asey to buy a new mirror and charge it to us— Asey, you'll just have to buy another new car and charge it to me. On my word of honor, I've never been half so embarrassed. Here."

He held out the pistol.

"I don't want it," Asey said.

"Neither do I. Take it, please. It's the second time in my life I ever fired a gun. The first time, I was in the army, and I shot off a sergeant's toe. That afternoon they made me a quartermaster, and I spent the rest of war in a storehouse. Asey, I *am* sorry— There's no use trying to tell you. You know I'm sorry. I shouldn't be at all surprised if you started thinking that Jane and I had designs on you!"

Syl coughed so energetically that Asey couldn't ignore him.

"This is my cousin, Syl Mayo," he said.

Charles shook hands with him. "How do you do? This is my daughter— Oh, you seem to know each other."

"He's the one," Jane said, "who fixes the Brickers' pump."

"You must come," Charles said cordially, "and fix ours the next time it gives out. It's a horrible contraption, and it gives out regularly on the Fourth of July and on Labor Day, and most of the weekends in between when we have guests. It works beautifully when we're alone, but the minute we have guests, it gives out, and causes—er—hideous situations.''

The corners of Syl's mouth turned up into a grin.

"That's most usually the time they always act up, when there's comp'ny. I'll be glad to take a look at your pump some day, Mr. Lennox. Just you give me a ring, any time.''

Asey looked at his cousin in some surprise.

Not only was there a genuine desire to be helpful indicated in the way Syl spoke, but also a genuine friendly warmth that was startling in comparison to his previous irony about the Lennoxes.

"That's good of you," Charles said. "Asey, I am frightfully sorry. Is there anything we might do to help you right now, or have you something you're looking into— By the way, Jane, would you be willing to pop back to the house and get my pipe?''

"You've got a pipe, right in your pocket.''

"Yes, dear. But get me another. Get me that briar on my study desk.''

"But—''

"Jane,'' Charles said, "I want to talk with Asey. Make it easy for me, and go get a pipe!''

"Oh, all right!''

Charles waited until Jane disappeared from sight.

"Asey, we're terribly upset about Irma. I called you a while ago, but your housekeeper said you were sleeping, and couldn't be disturbed. Asey, could you get to the root of this, please, for me? I feel a very definite responsibility, and I want things cleared up. I've no doubt that fellow Hanson and his police are doing their best, but from what the reporters said—"

"Had reporters already?"

"Just some local men, from the Fall River and New Bedford papers. I suppose we'll have more later. These were very decent, but from what they let fall, I gathered that anything over which Hanson presides is inclined to be a long-drawn-out affair. So, Asey, I'd appreciate your taking a hand. I want this cleared up. I think I owe that much to Irma."

Asey nodded. "I'll do what I can."

"Thank you. And— Well, can you get it over with quickly? I'm not thinking so much of ourselves, Asey, though God knows Jane is as nervous as a witch, and Kate's practically out of her mind, and William and Mary are breaking all the dishes, between them. I'm thinking about Jeff. And his campaign, and election, and all. It never occurred to me that his name might ever be mentioned in connection with this, but those reporters were going to see him when they left here."

"Why?" Asey asked.

"When I asked them," Charles said with a trace of bitterness, "they explained that he was the opponent of a murdered woman's missing fiancé, and that he was also a relative of the people who employed the girl. They were astounded when I asked them if they couldn't leave Jeff out of it. One of them said that Jeff was always news. So you see, I'd like to get this over with quickly."

"I see," Asey said.

"Now," Charles went on, "I'll go get Jane, and see if the two of us can manage to keep each other from going mad."

He turned away, and then came back to the car.

"I threw away the history of Quashnet this morning. I burned it up. I— Well, I didn't seem to want to go on with it."

Syl watched him as he walked along through the pine grove.

"I like him," he said. "I see what you mean, Asey. He ain't the sort that'd chase his secretary— You hear the way he said that his pump caused horrible situations? You knew just what he meant, an' yet he didn't say it." Syl chuckled. "Yup, I like him.

You might think first that he was sort of soft, he's so soft-spoken. But he can be firm, can't he? That girl minded him without any talk."

"He has a quiet way," Asey said, "of takin' the reins. He took 'em, if you noticed, right away from me. I had several things I wanted to bring up— Well, I can find out later."

"I liked the way he was so honest about shootin' off that gun. I guess I was wrong about him," Syl said. "You'd never suspect a man like him. He's just as nice, an' friendly, an' honest, an' above-board— What you say?"

"I said yes," Asey told him. "But I still wouldn't know a nicer way to polish anyone off, Syl, than by makin' a gay, blithesome accident out of it."

"Why, Asey!" Syl said in amazement. "How you talk!"

"Come on!"

Syl shook his head as he followed Asey around the corner and along the side of the sail loft. Sometimes, he thought, he couldn't understand Asey Mayo, at all.

"One minute," he murmured aloud, "you think one thing about somebody, an' then when someone agrees with you, you glower an' seem to think somethin' else! That shootin' was an accident, an' he admitted it— Where'd *he* come from?"

Syl pointed to the tall, gangly man in blue dungarees and a blue shirt, who was brushing out lobster pots on the shore in front of the loft.

The man turned and looked at them, and then turned back to his work.

"Hi," Asey said. "How long *you* been here?"

The man stacked one lobster pot on top of another before troubling to answer.

"Nour an' a half."

"Hear a shot?" Asey inquired.

"Yup."

"Not interested, huh?"

"Nobody shootin' at me."

Asey grinned and turned to Syl. "You ought to know this feller, cousin. You both got the same self-confident feelin' that if somebody shoots, it ain't at you."

"I think I do know him," Syl said. "I think I seen him at the Pochet Lodge. He's a Craddock."

"Another? It don't seem like there could be many more— Hey," he raised his voice, "is your name Craddock?"

"Yup."

"Which one are you?"

"Bert."

"My name is Mayo," Asey said. "I—"

"Yup. I know. You went to sea with my brother Eph, didn't you?"

"Why, I don't know as I did," Asey said.

"You did. Heard him say so. You were eight years old, an' it was your first voyage, an' he was mate, an' he tanned the hide off you for your plum duff. Had lumps in it. Soggy, too."

Asey threw back his head and laughed. "I *do* remember that. It was on the 'Betsey R.,' out of Wellfleet."

Craddock put down his brush, straightened up, and looked steadily at Asey.

"I guess you done pretty well for yourself since them days, ain't you?"

"Wa-el," Asey said, "I manage to make both ends meet, if that's what you mean."

"Get paid for all this detectin' you do, huh?"

"No," Asey said, "I can't say as I do."

"You mean folks don't pay you, or you don't ask nothin'?"

"I don't ask nothin'," Asey said.

"I found somethin' funny," Craddock said. "Maybe you might detect it for me."

"That so? What?"

Craddock hesitated. "No charge, huh?"

"No charge. What's your problem?"

Craddock walked over to where his coat was draped on the sand, removed something from underneath it, and walked back to Asey.

"Here."

He held out a miniature lavender china boot, about three inches high, in which a spiny cactus was growing.

"Now," Craddock said, "detect that."

"Where'd you find it?" Asey asked.

"Lobster pot."

"*In* a lobster pot?" Asey said. "Inside of a lobster pot?"

"Yup."

Asey turned the little boot around in his hand, and examined it curiously.

"Golly!" Syl said. "That's an awful queer thing to find inside of a lobster pot, ain't it?"

"I thought so," Craddock said. "Well, Mayo, if you're such a detector, how do you detect that?"

Asey shook his head.

"You got me, Craddock. I don't know."

"I guess it just goes to show," Syl said, "that you can't never tell what the sea'll bring forth, can you?"

"Nope," Craddock said. "Only this pot wasn't in any sea. It was on shore."

"Where?" Asey asked quickly.

"Inside the loft."

"Craddock," Asey said, "let me get this straight. You found this lavender boot with the cactus inside of a lobster pot, inside of the sail loft? Huh. Maybe I might detect this for you after all, if you'd unbend a little an' give me a few details. When'd you find it?"

"This mornin' earlier. I showed it to Lennox. I asked him what he thought."

"What did he say?" Asey inquired.

"He said it didn't surprise him. He said the way things was goin' around here, he wasn't a bit surprised to find a cactus growin' inside a lavender boot in a lobster pot. He said he wouldn't even be surprised if I found a lobster pot growin' inside of a cactus."

Asey chuckled. "Tell us more about this, Craddock. Did you take in those pots that's in the loft?"

"Yup. I started takin' 'em in on Thursday. I always take 'em in every year for Lennox. I pull 'em for him an' keep 'em baited, too. Well, I got some of 'em cleaned out and stacked up on Thursday. An' today, I got around to the rest. Really, I was aimin' to start in today on the boats. I thought my brother Dan'd help, but he's gone off— You know my brother Dan?"

"I missed him, I'm afraid," Asey said.

"Well, he's not one you can count on, you know," Craddock said. "You can't never tell about him. So when he didn't show up, I set out to clean the rest of these pots, an' put 'em inside, but first I had to move them that I'd put in, to make more room. An' this boot was inside of one of them."

"Just where?" Asey asked. "On the floor, or on one of the top ones, or in back, or where?"

Craddock's forehead wrinkled as he pondered the problem.

"I had two piles of three pots," he said at last, "an' one of two. Seems to me this was in the top pot of that two pile. I'm pretty sure it was."

Asey nodded. "Was it just like this, or did it have some sort of wrappin'?"

"Had fancy green wrappin' paper around it," Craddock said. "I took it off to see what was inside."

"An' tossed it away, huh? Syl," Asey said, "see if you can think where you'd blow to if you was a piece of fancy wrappin' paper, please. I'd like to see that paper."

Syl found it within ten minutes, over in the pine grove.

"There, now," Craddock said. "Now you got the whole story down to the wrappin's. Now you tell me why it's there in that pot this mornin', when it wasn't there when I put the pot in the loft on Thursday!"

"Wa-el," Asey said, "somebody bought this cactus in Boston—"

"How d'you know that?" Craddock demanded.

Asey pointed to the green paper. "See the monogram that's kind of watermarked on this wrappin' paper? Well, years ago when Bill Porter was courtin' his wife, he used to drive clear to Boston twice a week to get Betsey flowers from Brenn's. I seen hundreds of Brenn's boxes an' wrappin', an' they're all green an' got this monogram on 'em. So, somebody bought this cactus at Brenn's, an' left it here after you put the lobster pots in on Thursday."

"There!" Syl said with pride. "There! How's that for detectin' your cactus?"

But Craddock was far from satisfied.

"What'd anyone put it in a lobster pot *for*? That's what I want to know. I don't care much where it come from."

"If you had a cactus," Asey said, "would you be apt to put it in your pocket?"

Craddock guffawed. "An' run the chance of sittin' on it? No."

"Well, neither did this person that had it. Person put it out on what seemed to be a table— You said it was in the top pot of the two pile, didn't you?

That'd be about the right height for a table. But it fell down inside. Person couldn't get it without fishin' around an' undoin' the catch on the bait door—"

"Why didn't they? Why'd they think a lobster pot was a table, anyway? Who'd go around thinkin' a lobster pot was anythin' *like* a table, huh?"

"You might, yourself," Asey said, "if it was dark. You know this loft pretty well by day, but if you come here at night, don't you think that even you might mistake a pile of two lobster pots for a table, maybe, in the dark?"

"I wouldn't mistake a dozen lobster pots for anythin' but a dozen lobster pots," Craddock said. "If there's one thing you couldn't never fool me on, it's a lobster pot!"

"What Asey means," Syl said, "is that the pile of two pots is just about the same height as a table, an' if there's a table near 'em, someone might mistake the pots for it, at night! See?"

"I don't see," Craddock said, "as any person in his right mind'd come all the way from Boston with a cactus, just to lug it to this sail loft at night, an' drop it into a lobster pot they thought was a table! I don't see as any person in his right mind could even think of such a thing. But what I *do* see is why nobody pays you for detectin', if this's any sample of how you go at it— Hey, come back here with that cactus!" he added as Asey started to walk away. "That's mine! I found it—"

"In my loft." Charles Lennox had come up behind them so quietly that neither Syl nor Asey had heard him. "If Asey wants it, I think we'll allow Asey to have it. Asey, we are about to force ourselves to swallow a meal. Kate and I would be glad if you and your cousin joined us."

"Thanks," Asey said, "but I got work on hand. What kind of car did Irma Dine drive?"

"Jane's old Porter roadster. She bought it—"

"Model Y?"

"Yes, the one that slanted so. Are you sure you won't change your mind?"

"No, thanks." Asey ignored Charles's polite stare at the little lavender boot he held in his hand. "Be seein' you later. Come on, Syl."

"But, Asey!" Syl said as he trotted along in an effort to keep up with his cousin's strides, "ain't you goin' *into* the loft? Where you goin'? I thought you was goin' to try to find out—"

"Get into the car. Hustle!"

"But you said," Syl protested as the roadster started down the lane, "you said you wanted to find out if the girl'd been killed there, or not!"

"She was."

"Asey, it sounded like you said she *was!*"

"I did. I'd hoped for the Lennoxes' sake that she wasn't, but she was, an' I'm sure of it, an' now I'm goin' to prove it to my own satisfaction!"

"How can you tell?"

"From the cactus. It's clear as crystal. Now shush. I got to make sure."

At the intersection of the sail loft lane and the main road, Asey slowed down, turned to the right, and proceeded in the direction of Pochet at a pace which frightened Syl.

"What you crawlin' like this for? You feel all right, Asey?"

"Yup. Where's that tourist overnight camp? I thought it was right here."

"Just ahead. Beyond the billboard— But it's closed, Asey. I remember seein' the sign. Closed till June."

"I know. I seen the sign. I seen the Porter, too. It's parked behind one of the cabins in the second line— There, Syl! See? I noticed that radiator stickin' out when we come by. I always notice that model. It's one of the best Bill Porter ever made. Syl, this comes under the headin' of dumb luck. I was yearnin' to find out about this car business, but I thought we'd have to wild goose chase around Boston. Let's take a look."

"It's hers, all right," Syl said. "She didn't have the Lennox girl's initials taken off—see? J. L."

"The Lennoxes," Asey said, "are great hands for initialin' things. See if there's any bags in the rumble, Syl. Or stuff in the glove compartment."

A thorough search of the old Model Y revealed no luggage, and Syl dismissed with contempt the miscellaneous assortment of things he found in the glove compartment.

"Just junk. What's this all mean, Asey?"

"Means she drove down from Boston, Syl, parked her car here, an' went on foot to the loft. An' in her pocket was that flask she'd had fixed right away, for Slocum—"

"Think she was goin' to meet him at the loft, Asey? Because—"

"Let me think it out, Syl. She had the flask, an' she had the cactus—"

"What for?"

"Ssh! An' her pocketbook. I wish," Asey said, "I knew what was in that!"

"I thought she didn't have any," Syl said. "I thought that was why you an' the doc an' Hanson didn't know who she was, because she didn't have any pocketbook or things to identify her!"

"Right. But there's no keys in this car, Syl, an' women put car keys in their pocketbooks. You know that. Jennie's always losing hers in the depths of her bag. An' Irma Dine'd be bound to have her car license an' registration an' stuff, too. Yup, she had a pocketbook, an' it looks like what she had in her pocketbook was what someone wanted. Now, she goes to the loft, an' waits. Sure, she's got a pocketbook, Syl, an' maybe somethin' else. Hands are full. Puts cactus on lobster pot, gropin' around for the table top—"

"Whyn't she have a light? Who was she meetin' so secret?"

"Ssh. Somebody comes. Biff, an' that's that. They take her an' her pocketbook, they don't know about the cactus, so it gets left there. I don't see it Thursday night because I'm trainin' my light mostly on the floor. Come on, Syl. Got to check up on the cactus."

"I wish you would!" Syl said unhappily.

"She bought it in Boston at Brenn's. That store's right across from a big garage, Syl, an' it's right smack on her way down here. That's why I decided she'd come by car. She wouldn't have bothered goin' clear to Brenn's for a little cactus if she'd taken the train an' the bus down. Station's clear on the other side of town. Now, I'll stop in the village, an' you get out an' find out where that flower one lives. If only she's got a house cram full of plants an' aspidistras!"

"You're crazy," Syl said with conviction as they started back toward Quashnet. "What flower one? Who you talkin' about?"

"That one Jennie said gets all the flower prizes. Abby Hallet. The one Irma Dine used to board with. 'Member Jennie said she expected a card from the girl, but she hadn't got one. Girl forgot to write her. But when the girl gets her car to come back to Quashnet, she remembers Abby, an' stops in at Brenn's, an' buys the little cactus as a present and peace offerin'. See?"

"Mad," Syl said, "as a hatter. That's what you are!"

"It's the sort of thing," Asey continued, "that you'd only buy on impulse. The whole thing is impulsive and hurried, Syl. She hasn't any bags or luggage. She came back in a hurry on Thursday."

"If her car's been there since Thursday," Syl said, "why hasn't anyone seen it? Whyn't the Lennoxes see it when they drove past?"

"Maybe they did, Syl, but as far as they was concerned, Irma Dine an' her car was in Boston! They might have noticed it if it'd been left on the side of the road. But parked behind the cabin like that, nobody'd think much about the car, even if the sign said the cabins was closed."

Syl sighed.

"I still don't see, Asey, why that cactus made you so certain the girl was killed in the loft!"

"If she got the cactus as a present for somebody, Syl, an' carted it as far as the loft, then the girl got as far as the loft alive. Now don't say that someone else just threw the cactus away. With all Quashnet Bay starin' you in the face, you wouldn't throw a cactus into a lobster pot. Before you threw it away anywhere, you'd undo it to see what it was! Now," Asey stopped the car, "go into the drug store an' find out where this Abby Hallet lives."

When they drew up in front of Mrs. Hallet's house some fifteen minutes later, Asey took one look at it, and crowed.

Practically every inch of window space was filled with potted plants.

"I feel better!" Asey said. "Much better!"

Syl followed after him as he strode up the front walk and knocked at the door.

The angular woman who answered his knock frowned at him severely.

"What you want? You can't see the lady of the house."

"I wanted to speak with Mrs. Hallet," Asey began, "but you—"

"She's all gone to pieces an' in bed. All these people, knockin' an' bangin' an' askin' her a lot of questions!"

"Sorry," Asey said. "Could you tell me a couple of things, then, yourself? Does Mrs. Hallet have a lot of cactus plants?"

The woman looked surprised, but she answered him readily.

"Sixty-seven. I— She collects them."

"Thank you. An' did Mrs. Hallet go to the school dedication on Thursday?"

"Oh, yes. I— She was on the Woman's Committee. She sat on the platform."

"Thanks."

Asey grinned as he turned and walked back to the car.

He had a very definite suspicion that the angular woman was Mrs. Hallet, herself. He had heard his cousin Jennie get rid of too many salesmen with that line about the lady of the house.

Syl shook his head as he got into the roadster.

"I still don't see where any of this gets you!"

"You don't?" Asey said. "Well, Irma Dine bought a new cactus for Abby's collection, an' she got it as far as the loft. She was alive up to there. An' apparently she was dead afterwards. But Irma Dine didn't expect to run into any trouble there. She expected to meet someone, an' go along with that someone to the doin's at the school. That's why she carted the cactus along. She knew Abby'd be at the school, an' she'd see her before the evenin' was over. Syl, I find myself wonderin' about Henry Slocum again!"

"Well, I'm glad to hear that!" Syl said. "When I think how I tried since yesterday to get you to go to that place so's I could—"

"I know. Show me things and tell me things. Syl, is Henry Slocum puttin' on an act? Did Irma Dine expect to meet him at the loft? I plumb forgot about that gun he had in his overalls pocket—"

"Asey, she wasn't shot!"

"No, but a gun butt's nice to hit anyone with," Asey said. "Now I wonder. Could he have met her there, an' killed her, an' then put on that rantin' act for the Lennoxes? It doesn't seem right to me. But if he could make it seem that the Lennoxes and Jeff had plotted to keep him away from the school— Yup, Syl. It's possible that Slocum was tryin' to establish an alibi. That'd explain this disappearance of his. He can turn up an' claim that the plot deranged his mind, an' he's been havin' amnesia. I don't like it. It don't sound right to me. But I wonder if Slocum couldn't have been the one she set out to meet at the loft?"

"No."

Syl was so definite about it that Asey took his hand off the starter button and turned and looked at him.

"That's what I mean! No!" Syl said. "If Slocum went to the loft, he didn't go there to meet Irma Dine."

"Who do you think he was going to meet?"

"That's what I ain't sure about," Syl said unhappily. "That's why I keep wantin' you to go to Slocum's—all mornin' an' all noon an' half the afternoon, I been tryin' to get you to go there! An' you keep switchin' off. Or drivin' off! If you'll just come there, an'— Oh!"

Syl's cry was one of pure anguish.

For Asey had leapt out of the car, and was streaking toward the woods at the back of Abby Hallet's house.

TEN

~~~~~~

"ASEY! *Asey!* Asey Ma-yo!"

But Asey didn't even hear Syl's protesting, an-
guished yells as he raced past the Hallet house and
the Hallet barn into the woods where, for a brief
second, he had caught a glimpse of the man in the
dark felt hat.

And this time, the man in the dark felt hat was
not going to get away!

Asey stopped short as he came to a circular clearing in the woods.

There was no sight of that dratted fellow.

Not a trace of him.

Not even any sound of him running.

"Foxy, huh?" Asey murmured.

Very well, he thought. He would be foxy, too.
If the fellow wanted to hide among the bushes and
wait, he too would hide among the bushes and wait.
He had plenty of time.

"Asey!" Syl's plaintive voice came from the trees somewhere to his left. "Asey Ma-yo! Hey, Asey!"

Asey crouched down in the scrub oaks and watched while Syl trotted out into the center of the clearing and looked around.

He stood there for several minutes, with his hands planted firmly on his hips, and then he did exactly what Asey expected him to do. He started around the edge of the clearing, methodically stopping every few feet, listening and looking.

To the average observer, Syl's perusal would not seem very thorough, but Asey knew better. Few things would escape those beady eyes.

Asey lay flat and listened.

Then, as Syl slowly circled the far side of the clearing, Asey heard a crackling to his right.

Syl, diametrically opposite the sound, heard it too.

"Asey!" he called out pettishly. "Asey, what in tarnation are you doin', playin' games? Where are you? Where'd you go? What *ails* you!"

He started walking directly toward the place where the crackling sound had originated.

A second later, there was another noise which caused Asey to grin.

Felt Hat was up to his old habit of throwing things, as he had for Nosey on Thursday night.

And Syl was falling for it, too. He changed his course and walked to the right of where the original crackling sound had come from.

"Asey Ma-yo! What'n time are you doin'! What's the matter with you? Aha! I see you! You want to be chased, I'll chase you!"

Syl marched into the underbrush, and marched out of sight.

Asey lay quietly in the scrub oaks and waited.

Five minutes passed, and then another five.

Syl's yipping calls of "A-sey Ma-yo!" died away entirely.

Asey continued to wait. If Felt Hat hadn't seen him, maybe Felt Hat would be foxed by Syl's trailing away over the hills. He hoped so.

He had to take a firm grip on himself to keep from expressing his pleasure when, fully ten minutes later, he caught a fleeting glimpse of a figure slipping cautiously from tree to tree, not thirty feet beyond to his right.

It was old Felt Hat, gliding over the pine needles like a cat.

And it occurred to Asey in a sudden flash that Felt Hat was heading back toward the Hallet house!

Holding his breath, Asey squirmed around and watched.

The fellow was getting bolder, putting his feet down harder, and lengthening his stride.

Asey raised himself up on his elbows and watched. There was no question about it. Felt Hat *was* going to the Hallet house. He edged slowly around the barn, stood for a moment in the shadow of the elm by the kitchen ell, and then darted into the house by the kitchen door.

Asey's eyes narrowed.

Felt Hat hadn't darted in stealthily, he thought, like someone seeking the nearest refuge. There was the barn, if the fellow'd just wanted to take cover. Felt Hat had darted in without hesitation. He knew just where the door knob was, and which way to turn it, and which way to shove the door.

In short, it looked very much as though Felt Hat were pretty familiar with the angular Mrs. Hallet's kitchen door.

"Huh!" Asey said.

He got to his knees and surveyed the situation.

Now, when he could have utilized Syl as a distracting element at Mrs. Hallet's front door in order that he himself might slip in by the back door, Syl had gone with the wind. What he could have followed and where he could have followed it, Asey couldn't guess.

And there was practically no way of approaching

Mrs. Hallet's back door without being seen from the house. If he went to the back door, Felt Hat could slip out the front way. If he went to the front door, Felt Hat had only to pop back into the woods and play more tag around that clearing.

Asey sighed.

He had thrust Charles Lennox's old pistol into his pocket, but there would be little sense in marching to either door and brandishing that and demanding that Felt Hat come forth and give himself up and answer a bale of questions. The angular Mrs. Hallet would simply stall him, and give Felt Hat a chance to beat it.

And he didn't know that he wanted to engage in any shooting, anyway. It wasn't so much that Felt Hat had the advantage of being inside the house, Asey thought. The problem was that to stop Felt Hat, you'd have to stop him hard. And that would preclude the explanations that Asey wanted from him. He wanted Felt Hat alive.

Asey sighed again, and considered the elm tree by the kitchen ell.

Its branches made a great fan between the house and the barn. He could get to the rear of the barn without being seen. He could shinny up on the barn roof. He could get on that branch by the barn eaves, and, if he didn't break at least his neck in the process, he could make his way through the elm branches and land on the roof of the kitchen ell.

From there to the second story windows was child's play. And, Asey noted with gratification, the angular Mrs. Hallet was one of those thrifty souls who tacked mosquito netting over her windows instead of employing regulation screens.

"Mighty nice of you!" Asey said, and started out. The hardest part, he discovered, was neither shinnying up the barn nor navigating the branches of the elm tree.

The hardest part was the removal of a collection of six large potted begonias from the sill of the window he chose to enter. They had to be moved before he could get a leg over the sill, and even standing on tiptoe, Asey couldn't reach far enough into the room to deposit them on the floor without taking a chance of their dropping and making a noise. So, while he perched precariously on the ell ridge pole, he picked up the begonias one at a time and laid them on their sides in the wooden gutter.

Then he swung over the sill and into the room.

It was a bedroom with violently flowered wall paper and a vast brass bed on which a thin tiger cat was sitting and watching him suspiciously. His tense attitude said as plainly as any words that if Asey took one more step, he would regret it.

Asey stood still and stared back at the cat. If the animal chose to leap off the bed and rush down stairs miaowing, it might be just enough to arouse suspicion and set Mrs. Hallet and Felt Hat to investigating. And, Asey thought grimly, he had no intention of retreating and hanging on to that ridge pole with his teeth while the two of them conducted any tour of the house!

There was a round wooden button on the bureau. Asey reached over, picked it up, and tossed it on the bed. The tiger cat thrust out a paw, toyed with it, and purred. Then, turning his back on Asey, the cat resumed his nap.

Asey started on tiptoe across the grass floor matting.

He paused by the door.

On the wall at his left were three pictures. One was of Irma Dine, the same picture Slocum had on his office desk. This was inscribed, "Love to Aunt Abby from Irma," in the same flowing hand that Slocum's had been inscribed, "Love to Henry from Irma."

The next picture was of a boy with dark hair and the same thin nose and wide set eyes. It, too, was inscribed, "Aunt Abby from Carl."

The third picture had been cut from a rotogravure section and framed. It was the champion

Quashnet High School baseball team of a few years back.

One Carl Dine played shortstop.

"I wonder!" Asey murmured. "Now, I wonder!"

He slipped through the door and out into the hall.

The voice of the angular Mrs. Hallet floated up to him.

"I can't see a sign of no one, Carl! Can you? That car's still out front, but I can't see a soul around anywheres. There's nobody there! Now, for heaven's sakes, you come here an' tell me what you're doing down here!"

"You sure there's nobody, Abby?"

That must be Felt Hat, Asey thought. It had to be Felt Hat. And it was also the voice of the man who had said "Come in!" when he knocked at the cabin door the day before.

And, apparently, it was also Carl Dine, the brother of Irma Dine.

"I'm sure, Carl!"

"Look again! I don't understand where he went to!"

Asey grinned and thought of the hurt surprise his cousin Jennie would show when he got around to asking her why she had never mentioned this brother. He knew just what she would say. She would tell him that he hadn't asked about any brothers, he had only asked about folks, and a brother wasn't folks. Folks, to Jennie, began with one's father and mother and worked back into a maze of grandparents and great-grandparents. She never included the current generation as folks.

"There's nobody around, Carl. Stop your twitching and fidgeting, an' tell me what you're doing here! You must be crazy to come here! Don't you know what the judge said?"

"Yeah, but—"

"You know what he said would happen to you if you set foot on Cape Cod for five years! If anyone sees you an' tells on you, you'll have to serve that sentence, every day of it! What did you come here for? Are you crazy?"

"But I had to come, Abby! I been here since Thursday night—"

"Since Thursday?" Abby gave a little cry. "Carl! Since Thursday? Do you know about Irma?"

"I just heard a little while ago. Abby, if I get my hands on Slocum, I'll tear him apart! He did this, Abby! He—"

"How do you know? Where is he? Do you know where he is?"

"I don't know where he is, but I know he killed Irma! Listen, Irma got a phone call from him

Thursday afternoon, see? I was with her when she got it. At that boarding house she used to stay in when she went to business school. I was there waiting for her to get ready to go to the movies with me. It was about three-thirty, and I was trying to make her hurry, and he telephoned her, and—"

"Henry Slocum phoned her? What did he say? What did he want? How did he know where she was?" Abby demanded.

"I don't know! All I know is, he phoned her. She said yes, she'd go right back and meet him at the sail loft, and she understood— She was out in the hall, see, and I was in her room, but I heard all that. Then she hung up and came back and said to me that she had to go back to Quashnet in a hurry—"

"What for?"

"That's what I asked her, and she said she had to go, and she was in a terrible predicament, and then she began to cry."

"What was the matter? Are you sure it was Slocum who phoned her? What did she cry for?"

Asey could hear Carl Dine pacing around the floor.

"She wouldn't tell me, Abby. She told me to go along to the movies, and she'd be back the next day. But it's easy enough to guess what the matter was. It was Slocum. If she was in any kind of a predicament, it was all his fault, the dirty louse! She wouldn't be the first— Honest, Abby, what'd Irma see in him? I always told her he was a skunk! I always said he was a skunk even before he let me down like he did. He could have got me off that charge if he'd wanted to! But he wouldn't, he was so afraid of getting his good name spoiled! Talking to me about his good name—"

"I know, Carl! I know! But I want to hear about Irma!"

"Oh, it's all Slocum's fault, the dirty louse!" Carl said angrily. "He knew I didn't mean to steal Foster's car. He knew I just took it for a ride. I didn't mean to smash it up. Slocum knew that. He could have fixed everything. All he had to do was have a word with the judge. He's fixed up plenty. But he wouldn't do it for me, because he knew I didn't like him and was trying to make Irma stop going with him. He wanted to get me out of the way, so he let me take it—"

"Yes, yes, yes! So you had to take your suspended sentence. I know! But what was Irma doing at that boarding house, Carl? I thought she was going to stay with Isabelle!"

"She never said anything about Isabelle. She telephoned me Tuesday just after she came. She said she was going to be in town for a few days, and she hoped she'd have a chance to see me. She never said anything about staying with Isabelle! She didn't say anything about seeing Isabelle, even!"

"She didn't?" There was bewilderment in Mrs. Hallet's voice. "But, Carl, she was going shopping with Isabelle, an' to some concert— She was going to do all sorts of things with Isabelle an' that other girl, the one who lived in Dorchester. She told me she was!"

"She never said anything about either of 'em," Carl said. "I went over to see her Wednesday, but she wasn't in, and I thought she'd be out with those girls she knows. But she wasn't. She came back just as I was leaving— It was around nine-thirty. She was all alone, and she looked tired, and worried, and she had a lot of papers in a brief case with her. Said she'd been working—"

"What? Papers in a brief case, an' she'd been working? Now I wonder," Abby said, "do you suppose she was doing some work for Charles Lennox? What'd she be working on papers for? This was supposed to be her vacation!"

"Was it?"

"It certainly was! She came here one day last week, an' said her eyes hurt from working on that book of Lennox's, an' she was going to ask him for a vacation— You know, she'd planned to go back to Boston with the Lennoxes, an' she thought she'd take a rest first. An' the next day she told me she'd asked Lennox about the vacation, an' was goin' Tuesday, an' she did!"

"Well, gee, Abby," Carl said, "she didn't act like it was any vacation! She had more papers on Thursday. And she hadn't gone to any shows or anything. Because I asked her what movie we'd go to, and she said any one I wanted, she hadn't seen any. She didn't look like she was having any vacation. She looked awful worried and tired. It's all Slocum's fault, anyway, you can bet on that! I knew that when she started crying after he called her Thursday. If any girl knows him starts to cry, you don't have to guess what for!"

"Wouldn't she tell you anything, Carl?"

"Well, I asked her was it Slocum, and she cried and said it wasn't what I thought, and she didn't know what to do, but she'd have to go right back to Quashnet. I didn't want her to go, but she said she had to, and she wished she could talk with somebody, and I said she could talk with me. But she said she didn't mean me, and then she took all her papers and put 'em in her brief case, and gave me some money, and told me to go along to the movies, and she'd see me when she came back the next day, and to forget everything she'd said."

"An' you let her go off?"

"Well, what could I do, Abby? I couldn't come back with her, you know that! And I couldn't very well stop her, could I? Could anyone ever stop her when she wanted to do something? You ought to know they couldn't, Abby. You couldn't stop her, yourself!"

"But you came, didn't you?" Abby said.

"Yes, I did. After she left I got to thinking about Henry Slocum!" Carl was getting angry again. "I got to thinking what he'd done to me, and then I got to thinking about him and Irma, and I got a car from a man I know, and came down—"

"An' you been here since Thursday? What about your job?" Abby wanted to know.

"Oh, I quit that two weeks ago! I—"

"You quit this one, too?"

"Oh, the guy was a crab!" Carl said. "Fussing all the time because you couldn't account for every stamp. Docking you if you was just a few minutes late in the morning— Gee, you'd think it was a crime to be a few minutes late! Don't you worry, Abby. I'll get another job all right! I guess I can look after myself all right!"

Asey heard Abby's sniff.

"Carl, how old are you?"

"You know well enough! I'm twenty-two!"

"An' how many jobs you had?"

"Oh, I don't know! What's it matter? It's all Slocum's fault, Abby! It's all his fault! Everything's his fault! If he hadn't let me down like he did, I'd still have my job at the garage, an' I got along all right there, didn't I? Abby, we got to do something about Slocum! He was the one did this to Irma! This is all his fault, too! And if I lay hands on him, I'm going to tear him apart! I been trying to find him," Carl added. "I been trying to lay hands on him!"

"Where," Abby asked suddenly, "have you been since Thursday? What have you done since you come Thursday?"

Carl hesitated. "Oh, I been all over."

"Where?"

"Oh, all around. Provincetown. Pochet. All around."

"Carl, if—if you don't tell me just what you been up to since Thursday, you know what I'll do? I'll phone somebody an' tell 'em you're here!"

"You wouldn't dare!"

"I'd a lot sooner have you arrested for that car business," Abby said, "than for murder."

"What? What do you mean?"

"There's plenty of people don't think much of you," Abby said. "Plenty of people know how you hate Slocum. Plenty of people know all about the money your sister's paid, getting you out of trouble! And there's plenty might think you followed her down here from Boston for no good!"

"Aw, gee, Abby!" Carl said. "You don't mean that! Oh, my God! I never thought about— Oh!"

"You'd better tell me," Abby said. "You'd better tell me everything! Go on. Where'd you go first Thursday when you come?"

"To the sail loft. That's where Irma said she was going to meet him." Carl couldn't seem to get the words out fast enough. "But when I got there, there was just the Lennox girl—and Asey Mayo. I recognized him. He had a flash. I knew his voice, too. Sometimes he stopped at the garage for gas. I didn't think they knew I was there, but there was a dog, and I guess they caught on. Mayo slipped around the loft and nearly got me, but I got away. I'd left the car on that old lane, see, so Irma wouldn't know anything like about anyone following. Abby, didn't Irma tell you anything about why she went to Boston?"

"She's always been close-mouthed. You know she has."

"She might have been to you, because you always blabbed everything so! I suppose," Carl said, "that's why she told you that vacation story. She knew if she told you the real reason for going to Boston, you'd blab it around—"

"She was a pretty good sister to you, Carl Dine! Sending you money, getting you out of scrapes! Didn't you say she gave you money Thursday? Well, you remember those things! What did you do after you left the sail loft?"

"Well, I didn't want to be seen," Carl said, "so I drove around back roads. Then I drove past the school, and I heard someone say Slocum'd disappeared—"

"Carl, did Irma drive back here in her car?"

"Has she got a car? Did she have one?"

"Lennox sold her his daughter's old Porter. Didn't you know?"

"Gee, a Porter? Say, I wish I'd known she had a Porter! I'd have driven her down Thursday night whether she liked it or not! Where is it?" Carl asked anxiously. "Gee, a Porter!"

"I guess," Abby observed drily, "it's easy enough to see why Irma didn't never tell you about it! Go on with what happened on Thursday!"

"When I heard Slocum'd disappeared, I thought he'd most likely persuaded Irma to go away with him, see? I was burnin' up! I went down to Provincetown to see if I couldn't find 'em— I didn't think Slocum'd go far, because of the rally Friday.

I know all the places Slocum goes to, but he wasn't there, anywhere. I couldn't find 'em. I spent the night in Provincetown, and Friday— Gee, Friday was a day. First I rented a shack by the Pochet swamp from that real estate guy in Orleans—"

"Whatever for?"

"Well, I wanted to see what that skunk Slocum was up to. I was going to stick around and wait till he and Irma turned up. And I had to stay somewhere out of sight. I didn't dare come to you. I figured, if Slocum had married Irma, I'd go along back to Boston, see? But if he hadn't, I was going to tear him apart. I sneaked around the Lennoxes' to see if I couldn't find out something there, and then I went to Provincetown that night, and I heard that Slocum hadn't even gone to the big rally! And then Saturday—gee, that part was funny!"

"What part?"

"Well, the Lennox girl and Jeff Gage, they had this dummy. They got it out of the sail loft. I saw 'em. I was over there. Only I didn't know it was a dummy, first. I thought it was Slocum's body—"

Carl went on and told about the episode at the back shore. When he finished, he seemed reluctant to continue, and Abby had to threaten him again.

"Well," Carl said at last, "I went over to Slocum's— I'd been there before, to see if he'd got back. And on the shore road, I passed Asey Mayo, and he spotted me and followed me back to the shack, see? And—"

"Go on!"

"Well, I guess I lost my head. I was awful upset then, see, Abby. I'd seen Hanson and all the cops, and I got to thinking maybe something had happened to Slocum, and Irma'd done it. I thought maybe she might even have killed him. I thought—"

"What happened at the shack?"

"I knocked him out. With a frying pan."

Abby's reaction, Asey thought, was purely feminine. She wanted to know why Carl had used a frying pan.

"It was just there. That's all. I tied him up and left him— I was awful scared. I hadn't given my right name to the Orleans man, and the car plates were muddy, but I was scared. I thought first I'd killed him. I almost came here to you, then. I drove around, and then I went to Provincetown."

"You kept goin' there all the time," Abby said. "What for?"

Carl hesitated for almost a minute.

"I didn't want to go back to Boston," he said at last. "The car— You know, I told you I borrowed the car I came in? Well, I didn't. I stole it. I was afraid to go back to Boston in it, and I couldn't just get out and leave it, because on foot someone might recognize me around here, and—"

"That's enough," Abby said. "You're in more trouble in Boston, isn't that it? I thought so! Stealing cars, too, I'll wager! Is that so?"

Carl's answer was inaudible, but Asey gathered that it was in the affirmative, for Mrs. Hallet promptly read him a pungent lecture.

"The whole trouble with you," she concluded, "is that ever since you was the star on that baseball team an' had your picture in the paper, you thought you *was* somebody! An' you thought everything'd be just as easy as playin' ball! You don't get cars by stealin' 'em. You get cars by earnin' 'em, like Irma did. You're not a bad boy, Carl. You're just weak, that's all. An' I don't know but on the whole I'd rather you *was* bad. It's almost worse to get into trouble the way you do, just from bein' weak, than to get into trouble on purpose! Why didn't you explain everything to Asey Mayo, there at the shack, when you had the chance? What'd you knock him out for? Can't you see beyond your own nose? Didn't you think that sooner or later the police'd get you?"

Carl apparently shook his head, for Abby launched into another tirade.

"Honest, Abby," Carl said when she was through, "I didn't think what might happen till I heard two of Hanson's cops talking at the Chink's in Provincetown late last night. They were after a grey Ford. Mine. They didn't have the numbers, but they were talking about stopping any grey Ford driven by a man that looked like me. I didn't realize till then! And I hadn't only fifty cents left, and I couldn't go back to the cabin, and I didn't have much gas left, so I hid in the Truro woods all night. Abby, what'll I *do?* I saw Mayo driving along today, and I followed him. I was going to tell him. But I didn't dare. And I—I haven't had anything to eat. Abby, what'm I going to do!"

"Stop cryin'," Abby said, "an' let me think."

"Somebody ought to know it was Slocum she came to meet—but if I tell, they'll get me for being here! Just for being here. And then for everything else!"

"You're sure it was Slocum she was goin' to meet? Not Lennox?"

"It was that skunk, all right!"

"But are you sure? Did she say, 'Yes, Henry, I'll meet you at the loft,' or what?"

"She said, 'The sail loft, and I'll wait there.' Oh, and something about not being seen. I forgot that. And she said, 'I'll bring everything.' It was Slocum all right. She wouldn't meet Lennox there, would she? She'd meet him at the house!"

"What'd she meet *Slocum* there for? You know, Carl, I've heard some talk about her an' Lennox."

"Oh, but she liked them all! She said the Lennoxes were all swell to her! I tell you, it was Slocum! Abby, had I better try to skip somewhere, somewhere away, like New York?"

"You'll do nothing of the kind! You're going to tell Asey Mayo this whole yarn! Is his car still out there? Well, you're waiting till he comes back, an' you're telling him every word!"

"But I knocked him out!" Carl said. "He'll be good and sore!"

"If you're so sure it was Slocum she was going to meet, he's got to know it. An' if you hate Slocum as much as you claim, here," Abby said, "is your chance to do something about it! You—"

Asey got up from where he had been sitting on the top step, and leisurely came down the front stairs.

"Only two more things I want to know now," he said blandly, after they had recovered from their dazed astonishment at his appearance. "Where's the grey Ford? Out of gas? Okay. An' what was in the papers, d'you know? The papers your sister had in Boston?"

Ten minutes later, after convincing himself that Carl had no knowledge of the contents of the papers, and after receiving Mrs. Hallet's assurance that Carl would leave Quashnet only over her dead body, Asey walked out to his roadster.

There was no sign of Syl, which didn't disturb Asey at all. Probably, in his peevish mood, he had kept on walking to the main road, and thumbed a ride home.

Asey chuckled. He didn't blame Syl for being sore. He should have gone to Slocum's before, but things kept cropping up.

It was amazing, he thought as he started the car, how the more you found out of what you wanted to know, the less sure you were of your conclusions.

The events of Thursday night which had seemed so fantastic at the sail loft were beginning almost to be reasonable. He had everything cleared up but that infernal red wig.

The part that Carl Dine had played was all fitted in, he thought. That helped. And the method by which the body had been sent to the doctor's seemed pretty clear. That helped, too.

But where had that body been?

Asey found himself wondering once again about that refrigerated room at Slocum's store, and about the clerk Smith. And once again he dismissed the thought of both.

And, of course, there was the problem that seemed to have no solution.

Where was Slocum?

Where was Slocum? And what did the red wig mean? And where had the girl's body been kept?

It didn't make any difference, Asey thought, what order you asked those questions in. There they were, staring you in the face, three apparently unrelated problems.

What did the red wig mean? Where was Henry Slocum? Where had the girl's body been from Thursday night till Saturday night?

Asey gritted his teeth as he started along the Shore Road, past the new school.

He was almost in front of Jeff Gage's house when he braked suddenly and swung the roadster back toward the village drug store.

He could always have dropped in and put his burning question to Jeff Gage, but Asey knew from long experience that the clerk of a drug store had more accurate information at his fingertips than anyone else in a town. If he didn't know the answer, he would know who could supply it.

As he pulled up by the curb, Asey saw Bert Craddock ambling along the sidewalk ahead. Somehow he seemed taller and more gangling in his blue serge Sunday best than he had in the blue dungarees.

"Craddock." Asey leaned over the roadster's side. "Craddock, where are the ice houses in this town?"

"Huh?"

Asey repeated the question.

"What y'want to know for?" Craddock said.

Asey drew a deep breath.

"B'cause if y'want a piece of ice," Craddock continued, "my brother Abram's an ice man."

"Where's he keep his ice?"

"Y'don't have to go to no ice house. You can go right over to his house," Craddock pointed to the next street. "Lives in the yellow house with the green blinds. Just beyond the corner. What you want ice for this time of day?"

But Asey had already driven off.

Fifteen minutes later, Asey walked down the front steps of the yellow house with the green blinds.

Pausing on the bottom step, he turned and spoke to Abram Craddock, standing at the door.

"That's all there are in town? Just those four?"

"That's right." Abram Craddock was quicker than the other Craddocks with whom Asey had come in contact. "The ice house by Bound Brook's been empty for two years. No one could keep any body in that. I know that no body was kept in any of mine, either the two here in town, or the ones in Pochet or Weesit. I've been to every one of 'em every day since Thursday. Bleeker's ice machine broke at the fish freezer, and I've been supplying him. So that's the only other one, that one of Lennox's over at Cod Point."

"Thanks," Asey said.

"I understand," Abram Craddock said, "that you did some cactus detecting for Bert— Oh, yes, he's told everyone in town about that! I hope this ice house detecting turns out to be more successful. But Lennox's is the only one I can think of for you to detect."

Asey's detecting at Lennox's ice house on Cod Point turned out to be so successful that Asey pinched himself at the scene he interrupted there.

ELEVEN

ASEY knew that Charles Lennox had heard his roadster drive up and stop in front of the ice house.

He knew that Charles Lennox knew that he was standing there now in the wide doorway, watching him.

And yet Charles Lennox continued tugging at Henry Slocum's body, moving it to the right side of the front seat of Slocum's own car which had been driven inside the half-empty ice house.

At last, Charles stepped from the running board and faced Asey.

Each man waited for the other to speak.

"Well?" Charles said at last.

"How long have you known that his body was here?" Asey asked.

"I just found it. I've been thinking and wondering where Irma's body could have been kept. The ice house just occurred to me a few minutes ago, when I passed by here with Nosey. I walked back and opened the door. That's all."

"An' you don't know nothin' more about it than that?"

Charles shook his head. "I haven't been here ten minutes. But I think he's been here some time."

Asey walked past him into the ice house. Then he went back and got a flashlight from his roadster and returned.

Slocum was dressed in green and white striped pyjamas, and he had been killed, Asey guessed, exactly as Irma Dine had been killed, by a blow on the head.

"How?" Asey answered Charles's quiet question. "He was slugged with a blackjack."

"What do you suggest that I do?"

"What," Asey returned, "were you doing when I come?"

"In a moment of what I can only describe as panic," Charles said, "I was moving him. I had some notion of getting in behind that wheel and driving this car off my property. I think it was a natural panic. I think I understand now why Jane has acted so strangely since Thursday night. I think I know now how she felt after stumbling over that sleeve. I didn't understand till a few minutes ago what she meant when she said she was completely unnerved."

His voice was steady, but Asey was aware that its

steadiness was due only to Charles's infinite self-control.

"You," Charles continued, "might possibly have succumbed to the same temptation to drive that car and the body somewhere else, if you were in my place, and if Henry Slocum's body were found in your ice house. I'll even admit that I *should* have driven it away, if you hadn't happened along. It was bad enough when Irma was killed in the sail loft. But this! Asey, I've always felt, all along, that *he* was responsible! I thought that he'd killed Irma!"

"Why?"

Charles leaned back against the doorway.

"It's not an easy thing to explain, Asey. But up to the time that Slocum knew Kate and the rest of us, there were many things of which he wasn't aware. I don't pretend to know if the things he learned from us were good or bad. But they changed his standards, I think."

"You mean, he was outgrowin' Irma?" Asey remembered that Jeff had said something like that, something about Slocum's friends resenting his acquaintance with Kate Lennox, and thinking that he was getting high hat.

"I think there were things about her which were

beginning to irritate him. I think that's why Irma was so anxious to improve herself. She realized the change in him, and she wanted to climb with him. I always felt they'd do well together. She steadied him, and he gave her the stimulation she needed to climb out of Quashnet. But I know they've quarreled lately. I've come on her crying once or twice. I gathered it had something to do with Slocum, but I didn't inquire into it."

"You really knew quite a lot about Slocum, didn't you?" Asey said. "In spite of all your chatter about— What was his name, with the teeth? The lama?"

"Larrabee? Well, he always did remind me of Larrabee, physically," Charles said. "Are you married, Asey? No, I thought not. If you were, Asey, you'd realize that sometimes if you make light of a situation, the situation becomes light. Jane's spent a harum-scarum summer playing around with Ty, and it was good for her. Emmet and Anise—the other children—have always cramped Jane, and I think she needed this horseplay. But horseplay doesn't take up the mind, and Jane was beginning to focus that active mind of hers on Henry Slocum and her mother. So I have been making light of Henry Slocum, and forgetting his name. I didn't wish Jane to cause her mother and Henry Slocum and Irma any unpleasantness if it could be avoided."

Asey nodded.

"Jane," Charles went on, "is at an age where she likes things to be dramatic. Well, I didn't care to have any dramatics."

"You knew," Asey said, "that there'd been gossip?"

"About Kate and Slocum? Certainly. Kate," Charles said thoughtfully, "would have made a much better bank president than I did. She goes at things, if you know what I mean. If she learns to fly, she doesn't stop till she gets her pilot's license. She's the sort of woman who goes out and pickets. And of course people gossip about her. They always have, ever since she was a suffragette. You should have heard my own bank directors, when she stumped the state for Roosevelt!"

Asey grinned.

"I see your point," he said.

"I knew you would. Lately it's seemed to me she's been even more vigorous, but life can be dull for a woman when her children grow up, and I'm glad Kate finds things to do."

"Tell me about this vacation of Irma Dine's," Asey said. "Did she say why she wanted one?"

"No, but the history of Quashnet was tiring in spots. I understood why she might want a rest."

"Did you give her any work to do for you in Boston?"

"No. Oh, yes, I did say that if she visited the State House, she might drop in and check on a couple of dates. But I didn't make any issue of it. Why?" Charles asked.

"Just wondered. You know where she was staying?"

"I don't think I asked," Charles said. "I assumed she'd stay with relations or friends. She wasn't an awfully communicative girl. Asey, don't you think that Slocum killed her, and then was killed in turn by someone else?"

"I think someone hoped," Asey said, "that we might think so. I think that was why Irma Dine's body was kind of pointedly brought to light, so Slocum would be suspected. I even kind of wonder if, maybe, after some of the hue and cry had died down, that someone wouldn't have come here some dark night an' driven this car into the nearest pond. Who has a key to this place, or don't you lock it?"

"It's not locked, ever. We own the pond beyond, and if there's ice, Craddock cuts it for us. Of course in the old days before we had electricity, we used this exclusively. Asey, when was he killed?"

"The doc can tell you better than I."

Asey turned and started for his car.

"Wait, man!" Charles said. "What shall I do about this—about him?"

"I'd suggest you call Hanson."

Charles looked at him for a moment. "Asey," he said, "on Thursday night, I sat in my study and read about Ethan Pilcher, and Quashnet. I never stirred from the house until I went out hunting Slocum with you and Jane. I want you to know that, and I hope you believe it— Oh!"

"What's the matter?"

"I just noticed our cupola flag go up," Charles said. "Ty and Jane have an intricate system of signals, with that flag and the lights. You can see either all over town, you know. Asey, I hope you believe me. I'm still embarrassed about that shot that came so near to you— I feel that you're suspicious of me."

"What," Asey said suddenly, "would you say if anyone asked you to sum up Henry Slocum?"

"He wasn't unintelligent," Charles spoke without hesitation, "and he was very shrewd. He wasn't without a sense of humor, although it was a little bucolic for my taste. I understand he used to drink a lot, but he seemed to have cut it out lately, and he always behaved himself like a gentleman in my house, up till Thursday night. I think," Charles added, "that he'd have given Jeff a run for his money, and I'm not at all sure that he'd have cast any such blight as Jeff predicted if he won. I mean, grass wouldn't have grown in the streets of Quashnet or the highways of Cape Cod. Jeff always claimed he was planning deals, but I've known Jeff to swing a deal or two."

"Doc Cummings," Asey said, "told me that Slocum was brash. Jeff said he was a scheming, over-ambitious thing. Smith, his clerk, said he was a drunk. Your daughter called him Abe Lincoln in Illinois."

Charles smiled. "Each man carries a yardstick," he said, "with which to measure the world. It will be interesting to observe Hanson's yardstick when I tell him about this. He'll have me arrested within the hour. Asey, did you ever find out who the man in the dark felt hat is? Has anyone *ever* caught sight of him?"

"He's Irma's brother."

"Carl? What's he doing around here?"

Asey summed up Carl's part in the events of the last few days.

"That fellow," Charles said, "has a positive genius for putting his foot into things. He's not a bit vicious, but he has a movie mind— You know, if anyone dropped an ash tray in the movies, Carl would never think of its falling down unless he was shown it on the floor. And he was around all that time— Dear me, Hanson'll be hard put to pick between us, won't he? Where are you going now, Asey?"

"To Slocum's house," Asey told him. "I been tryin' to get there since yesterday, but this time, I'm goin'. I want— Hey, what's Nosey got?"

"A rat," Charles said. "A— No, by George, Asey, he's got the red wig! I haven't seen that since Thursday! Nosey, come here! Come on, boy! That's right. Give it to me. Good dog! Here, Asey. It looks a little shopworn. Ty was trying to make him find it after lunch today— I had a suspicion at first that it might be some prop of his or Jane's, but they both swore to me that it wasn't. D'you pretend to understand the significance of this wig?"

"Nope," Asey said, "but I got two questions answered out of three in the last hour, an' I'm goin' to go to work on this. Get in, you an' Nosey, an' I'll drive you back to the house."

Charles Lennox was silent as they drove up Cod Point Lane.

"Asey," he said, "I'm glad that you've relented enough about me to drive me home. You had me worried a few minutes ago. I was afraid you didn't believe me. Asey, what shall I do if Hanson—if he suspects Kate—or—or Jane?"

"I think," Asey said, "you might reasonably figure that Irma Dine an' Slocum was both killed by the same person. I think the girl was killed before seven twenty-seven on Thursday evenin', because that was when Jane run out in front of my car, and my car clock's been stopped at seven twenty-seven ever since. And at that time, your wife was already at the school for the dedication, wasn't she? Well, that lets her out."

"But Jane!"

"Jane was at the loft, yes," Asey said. "But until you establish when Slocum was killed an' do a little delvin', you can't hardly make any arrests, can you?"

Charles sighed his relief.

"I suppose I could have thought that one out, couldn't I, instead of feeling that you were letting the Lennoxes face this blitzkrieg alone. Unnerved is the word, all right! Thank you, Asey!"

Once again Asey sped along the Cod Point Lane, around the foot of Quashnet Bay, and up the Shore Road, past the new school and the old Town Hall, and the ball field, and Jeff Gage's house.

Things, he thought, were getting on.

He knew now where the girl's body had been kept. It had been kept in the Lennoxes' ice house until someone decided to send the body to the doctor's on Saturday.

And he knew where Henry Slocum was, and had been. Probably he had been there in the ice house since Thursday. That was an item, Asey thought, that he'd try to settle, right now at Slocum's.

Now if he could only make some sense to that infernal red wig!

At the end of the Shore Road, Asey turned off on the rutted lane leading up the hill to Henry Slocum's house, but before he had covered ten yards, he had to brake and swing to the left to avoid driving through a vast, slough-like puddle of water and mud that completely obliterated the ruts at the foot of the slope.

He never knew quite what impelled him to stop the car and consider that puddle so intently. But, as he gazed thoughtfully at its dimensions, it occured to Asey that there had been no rain since Wednesday afternoon.

And there was a culvert there, too, that continued from the Shore Road and took care of the overflow from the brook beyond.

Asey got out of the car, circled the puddle, and investigated the culvert.

The puddle, he discovered, was intentional.

The culvert had been stopped up with stones

taken from the low stone wall beyond, thus forcing the water to run over the road. Some attempt had been made to remove the stones, but enough debris had collected behind them to keep the culvert blocked.

"Huh!" Asey said.

He looked up the hill, and circled around the puddle again.

It was large enough now so that any driver would cut around it, as he did. But even if the puddle were smaller and not so noticeable, the worst it could do to any car was to get it stuck. A driver coming down the hill would brake on those deep ruts. A driver going up would probably shift before he got to the ruts.

No matter how you considered it, that man-made puddle would never cause any fatalities to anyone in a car.

And no one on foot, Asey thought, was going to walk into a mud puddle.

He strolled around the puddle twice, and then he caught sight of the string tied around the base of a scrub pine tree. It was just a plain piece of ordinary twine that had been broken off about a foot from the knot, but it explained a lot to Asey.

"Huh!" he said again, and walked slowly up the hill.

There were two cars outside Slocum's weather-beaten Cape Cod house. One was the Lennoxes' big black sedan, and the other was Jane's gleaming Porter Twelve.

Asey paused and looked at the house, mentally noting that it had neither phone poles nor electric poles. It was an old-timer, all right, he thought, and he could tell from where he stood just what it would be like inside. There would be a shed or two and a rudimentary kitchen in the ell, and beyond there would be a dining room with wainscoting and at least eight doors leading from it. Two doors would lead to the front rooms on either side of the front door with the fan glass. Two doors would lead to bedrooms, two to cupboards or pantries, one door would go up to the attic, and one would lead to a circular cellar under the dining room.

He tried to track down some specific fact that might justify his feeling that he had been here before, and then he remembered that this was the old Esty house. He had come here years before with his mother, to a wedding or a funeral, he couldn't remember which. The family had either died out or moved away, but he remembered that Elisha Esty had always been known as Squire Esty.

He felt a tug at his sleeve, and turned around to find Syl beside him.

"Don't you never listen, Asey? I said your name three times! Asey, you know what those folks done?"

"Who?" Asey said. "Hey, I remember. It was a wedding I come to. One of the Esty girls. She married one of the Freemans. There was seventeen kinds of cake, an' my mother spanked me when I got home for disgracin' her an' eatin' so much. Golly, I don't know *how* long ago that was. It was before I went to sea— What you say, Syl? What folks?"

"Sometimes," Syl said, "you're enough to drive a man to drink! Will you come out of this fog an' listen to me? Are you listenin'? Well, Jeff Gage, an' Mrs. Lennox, an' Jane an' that Bricker boy, they're all inside there! An' they burned up those notes! If you'd only got here when I tried to make you come, this wouldn't never have happened. Where'n time did you race off to, anyways? Now the notes is gone!"

"What notes?"

"You remember, before you went streakin' off there by that Mrs. Hallet's, I was tryin' to tell you that Slocum might of gone to the sail loft to meet someone, but it wasn't the Dine girl?"

Asey nodded.

"Well," Syl said, "I was goin' to tell you about the notes, then. I wanted to wait an' show 'em to you, because it didn't mean much just tellin' you.

There was two notes in there, Asey. One was signed Kate— That's Mrs. Lennox, ain't it? An' it said, 'Meet me at seven, Kate.' An' the other said, 'Meet me at sail loft before school. Jane.' That must of meant on Thursday night, Asey, see? She must of meant the school dedication. An' now they're all burned up!"

"Why'd you let 'em do it?" Asey asked.

"How could I stop 'em, Asey? I was out there in the kitchen, lookin' around, an' Jeff Gage picked up them papers from the desk there, an' next thing I knew, he had 'em burned! I seen him take out his cigar lighter, but I never thought but what he was goin' to light a cigar. He had a cigar in his mouth."

"Jeff burned 'em?"

Syl nodded. "N'en he tossed 'em into the fireplace, still burnin', an' everythin' in it went up before I could get my mouth open. N'en Mrs. Lennox said she guessed that was best, an' Jeff said he hoped so, an' Jane said she thought it was the best idea she an' Ty Bricker'd had yet. You couldn't rightly say that *Jeff* done it, Asey. They all seemed to of known he was goin' to. What you goin' to do about it all, Asey?"

"I don't see," Asey said, "as there's anythin' I can do. Syl, this was the Esty place, wasn't it? How'd Slocum come to own it?"

"I asked around town about that yesterday," Syl
said. "Seems that there was two Esty sisters livin'
here. That Mrs. Freeman, an' another, an' I guess
they was poor as all get-out, an'—"

"Poor? I thought the Estys used to own all the
town," Asey said. "An' one of 'em married into the
Freemans, an' they never was poor!"

"I guess it was ownin' so much land that was the
trouble," Syl said. "All the taxes, an' nothin' much
comin' in. They sold it in driblets, but they never
got much for any of it— The Lennox place at Cod
Point used to be Esty land, Asey, long ago. An' they
owned all where the golf club is, too. Anyways, I
guess they was up against it, an' from what I heard,
they'd have starved to death if it hadn't been for
Slocum. He give 'em all the credit they wanted, an'
looked after 'em, an' they left him this place when
they died. Guess it was mortgaged up to the hilt,
too."

"Syl," Asey said, "what's your opinion of Henry
Slocum?"

"I don't know," Syl said. "I didn't know him. I
never thought of votin' for him, because I always
vote for Jeff. But I guess there's a lot of folks that
like him. I guess he's tried to do his best for the
town, an' help people out when he could. Mrs. Lennox an' Jeff was just talkin' about him, though, an'

I guess Jeff doesn't think so much of him. They kind of had an argument about it on the way over here. They brought me over here in her car— Say, where *did* you go to, Asey, streakin' away like you did?"

"Where'd *you* go?" Asey countered.

"Oh, I kept followin' somethin' I thought was you," Syl said in disgust, "an' it turned out to be a rabbit! N'en I yelled around for you, an' then I come out on the main road— That was where Mrs. Lennox an' Jeff picked me up. They drove by, an' then they backed up an' Jeff asked if they could take me anywheres. They was on their way to the soft ball game. Quashnet Legion versus Wellfleet, an' they asked if I wanted to go, an'," Syl added defensively, "I thought I might as well spend my time there as wanderin' around chasin' rabbits!"

"Kind of sore at me, huh?"

"Well, who wouldn't be? Say, they got a good pitcher for Wellfleet, Asey. Fellow that opened the new gas station. Well, anyway, we seen the game, an' then Jeff treated me to a sandwich at Johnson's, an' then I said I guessed I'd come over here. I come to the conclusion," Syl said, "that it was easier to stay right here an' wait for you to get around to comin' here than to try an' keep up with you gettin' here. They said they'd drive me over, so they did, an' they went in. An' a few minutes later Ty an' Jane come in her car— An' you know what Ty Bricker had? He had an armful of pants!"

"What's that!" Asey said. "Say that again!"

"Ty had an armful of pants," Syl repeated obediently. "Asey, I wish you'd go in an' *look* at things in that house before anyone tampers with anythin' else! There's a wash tub of dirty water in the kitchen, right by the stove— That's where Slocum took a bath, I think. You can see his footmarks on the newspaper on the floor beside it, where he stepped out. Thursday's paper, too. An' there's brilliantine, an' a bottle of witch hazel, an' all. I figured that was where he set out to get dressed up for that shindig at the school Thursday—but you know what? Out in the shed is his suit, Asey. An' I want you to see that suit. It's—"

"I know," Asey said. "All mud an' dirt. An' it smells of whiskey, don't it?"

"How'd you know that?" Syl demanded.

"He got all snaked out for the school dedication, an' then he went outdoors," Asey said, "an' then— Huh. Let's get this straightened out!"

He marched into the house and into the dining room.

Mrs. Lennox and Jane and Jeff and Ty Bricker all looked startled at his sudden entrance. And all of them, Asey thought, looked sheepish.

"Bricker," Asey noticed that Ty had the same twinkle in his eye that Bill Porter used to have when he was younger, "Bricker, did you take the keys out of both them cars, Jane's an' Slocum's?"

"Sir?"

"You heard. An' just what time did you go to New York on Thursday?"

"It's all my fault," Jane said quickly. "I misled you. I—"

"I'm talkin' to Bricker, Jane," Asey said.

"Yes, sir. I took the keys. I was going to come and make a clean breast of it to you. I told Father, and he said if I didn't, he would. You see—"

"You took the keys out of both cars, an' plugged up the culvert, didn't you? N'en you tied a string to a pine tree, an' crossed over an' waited in the bushes opposite, holdin' the other end of the string. Right? You knew Slocum hadn't any phone, an' he'd have to set out on foot for the school. N'en when he come stormin' down the hill, you just jerked up your end of the string, an' let him trip smack into the puddle you'd made. That right? N'en what, did you throw whiskey on him?"

"What on earth—" Jeff began.

"Wait," Asey said. "I want to get at this. What happened then, Bricker?"

"Yes, sir. I had a bucket full of water, laced with a quart of De Silva's worst," Ty said. "I think the fall stunned him, or his breath got knocked out, because he lay there very conveniently while I poured the mess over him. Then I threw the bucket down towards the Shore Road, and raced up here—"

"An' swiped all his pants?"

"Yes. He stormed around down there for a while — I think he followed the sound of the bucket. I was over the hills and far away before he got back up to the house, here—"

"You see, Asey," Jane's face was crimson, and she avoided her mother's eyes, "I'd put on the cupola lights, and Ty saw them, and knew that meant for him to go whole hog, with the whiskey and the pants and everything. You see, I was going to talk to Mother, and make her promise to—to cut out all this campaigning around and all, and if I couldn't get anywhere with her, I was going to see if I couldn't make Dad take a hand. And if I couldn't, I was to put on the cupola lights, and Ty would give him the works. If Mother or Dad had only listened to me, we'd just have let him get muddy, and left it at that. We thought he'd be excited enough if he had to give his speech in his old clothes."

"Jane!" Kate Lennox said. "You—you and Ty did that? Asey, they really didn't do that, did they?"

"Looks," Asey said, "like they did. So Slocum come back to the house, here, an' peels off his muddied best clothes, an' then finds he hasn't anythin' to cover himself with— Huh. I understand them flappin' overalls now!"

"The poor boy!" Kate Lennox said. "And he'd never dare be seen— And no one would believe but what he was drunk! Oh, Jane, how could you have!"

"That's not all, Mother," Jane said. "I wrote a note, and Ty stuck it under the windshield wiper of the roadster when he first came. That was the note you couldn't understand about just now. The one about meeting me at the loft. We decided he'd never dare show himself, and we hoped to lure him to the loft."

"Jane, what for?"

"Well," Jane's cheeks were flaming, "if you want to know, I had a run-in with your precious Henry! What— Well, what you'd call an unpleasant experience! And I'd stood just about enough of having him around the house, and people talking about him, and you—"

"Why didn't you let me know?" Kate said. "Oh, Jane! Why didn't you tell me! Oh, my dear—"

"Why," Jeff said to Ty, "didn't you tell *me?*"

"Well, sir, we decided we probably could humiliate him a lot better than you could," Ty said. "You see, Jane went to the loft to meet me. We were going to wait outside in the hope that he'd show up, and then Jane was going to speak to him, and then scream, and then I was going to come rushing up and give him what he deserved. If he didn't come to the loft, we were going to drive around and find him, and go through some sort of act, and then—"

"An' then," Asey said, "make a juicy story out of it that wouldn't do credit to Slocum. What about Jane's car? How'd that get back?"

"Oh, I came back for that," Ty said. "I waited on the next hill till I saw him starting out in those overalls, and then I put his key back in his car, and drove Jane's car off— I meant to go straight to the loft, but I stopped at our house to leave those pants, and Father grabbed me and made me drive him to see a man in Provincetown, and then he made me drive to New York. I kept trying to duck, but Father was adamant. I never knew a man to be so stubborn. Wouldn't let me stop or phone, or anything. When he insisted I drive him to New York, I made him drive our car to Cod Point, and I drove Jane's Porter, but there wasn't anyone there. I put the car in the garage, and went on with Father. I was worried about Jane down at the loft, and I wanted to go there, but Father was in such a sweat—"

"Okay," Asey said. "That's enough so I see what happened on Thursday night. No wonder Slocum seemed out of his head when he finally got to the Lennoxes' that night! No wonder he had a gun in his overalls pocket! If you'd done any of that to me when I was about to make the speech of my life, I'd have gone out with a brace of shotguns! And the cussedness of pourin' that whiskey over him— No one would ever have gone any farther than the smell! He wouldn't have dared be seen, or go anywhere, or anythin'! Huh. So your note was a lure, Jane. Mrs. Lennox, what about your note that got burned?"

"I left that here Thursday morning," Kate Lennox said. "I was going to meet him at the school at seven, to hear his speech over once again— How— how did you know about that? About the burning?"

Jeff chuckled. "I told you I bet that someone would have read the notes! Asey, where can Slocum be? Have you any idea what's happened to him?"

"Uh-huh," Asey said, as he went to one of the

bedroom doors. "Yup. After all that harrowin' experience Thursday, an' lashin' out at you an' the Lennoxes, he come back here, wishin' he hadn't, an' went to bed in striped pyjamas. N'en—not very long later, I'd say, to judge from the looks of that bed—n'en he heard a noise outside. He went out to investigate it. You can see where he would, after what he went through that night. An' I'd say that someone was waitin' for him by the ell door. I don't think he knew what hit him any more'n the girl did. N'en—"

"Asey, you mean he's dead!" Kate Lennox said.

"Uh-huh. An' then," Asey said, "someone put him in his own car, an' drove him off. Over to your ice house, Mrs. Lennox, an' drove the car inside. An'—"

"Oh!" Jane said. "Oh! Oh, Mother, isn't that awful! Oh, if only we hadn't done this, Ty! Why did you have to *see* those cupola lights! Why did I put them on! Why did we think of any of this— How could we have ever thought that any of it was funny! How—"

"Which reminds me," Asey said, "what was you signalin' when you run up the flag a while ago? I noticed that just after I happened on the body."

"Oh, that?" Jane said. "Oh, that didn't mean anything, Asey! Ty and I were just saluting crazy

Dan Craddock. We always do. You know Dan, don't you?"

"Dan," Asey said, "seems to be another Craddock I missed."

"He's the oldest of the lot," Jane said, "and he's a bit quaint. Spends all his time paddling around the bay—"

"Who's this?" Jeff interrupted, as another car drew up outside. "Who's coming?"

"Hanson," Asey said. "I'll go see what he wants. I—"

"Wait," Jane said anxiously, "you don't understand about the flag, and saluting Dan, and all. He paddles around the bay, picking up flotsam and jetsam, stuff like—"

"Like driftwood," Ty said, "and bits of boards and crates. And orange peel. Anything he happens to see floating around. He's always out there in the bay. He's been scavenging around the bay for years. And—"

"And we always salute him," Jane said, "if we happen to notice him when he goes by the inlet at our place. Sometimes I've put on the cupola lights for him, if I've seen him paddling around on a moonlight night. Please don't think that flagging meant anything more, Asey! We were just saluting old Dan. Isn't that true, Ty? It didn't have a thing to do with our coming here just now, did it?"

"We came to bring back those pants," Ty said. "We meant to come earlier, but—"

He broke off as Hanson swaggered into the room.

Asey's eyes narrowed as he watched that swagger.

He knew it, and what it meant. He had seen it many times before.

It was what Dr. Cummings was accustomed to refer to as Hanson's Arresting Swagger, and it meant that Hanson was going to start waggling his forefinger at somebody, and announce that they could come along with him.

Asey was prepared to see the forefinger waggle towards Jane.

But he never expected Hanson to point at Kate Lennox.

TWELVE

"OKAY, Mrs. Lennox," Hanson said. "You can come along with me."

"Hanson," Asey said quickly before the others could speak, "wait! Wait just a sec! Have you seen Charles Lennox? Do you know about Slocum's body?"

"I know," Hanson said. "I seen it. Lennox called me."

"But look here, Hanson," Asey said, "don't you think you better pause an' reflect? The Dine girl was killed on Thursday evenin'—"

"I know. And Mrs. Lennox is supposed to have been at the school dedication. But she wasn't. She wasn't there all the time. She left, twice, in her car. And one of my men saw a note here about her meeting Slocum at the loft—"

"You're all wet!" Jane said hotly. "That was *my* note about the sail loft! Mother was going to meet Henry Slocum at the school at seven, and she left a note for him about it, but nothing was ever said about Mother going to the sail loft to meet any-one, ever! And before you start arresting people, you'd better check up on these things and get 'em straight!"

"Where are the notes?" Hanson asked at once.

Nobody answered him.

"Where *are* they?"

"Well," Jane said, "if you want to know, they're both burned up!"

"What? Who burned them?"

"Hanson," Jeff said, "those notes are of abso-lutely no significance, and they're nothing to get excited over. I burned them up myself. And I think, if this is any example of your detective work, that you had best go quietly away and start all over again!"

"Yeah?" Hanson was thoroughly angry. "Well, it won't do you any good, destroying state's evi-dence! Because she left that school twice. Didn't you, Mrs. Lennox? Didn't you leave the school twice?"

Kate Lennox nodded.

"Yes," she said calmly. "I left, twice. Dear me, Lieutenant, I can't tell you how relieved I am— I mean, I had this horrible feeling that you might ar-rest Charles, or Jane. Really, Jane, I've been awfully worried about the two of you."

"Where'd you go?" Hanson was at the barking stage, Asey noticed.

"Well," Kate said, "I left once to come over here, and then I was afraid that Henry'd gone around by the village, so I turned around and went back to the school. Then, the other time I went out— Was that while Manuel Rosa was talking, Jeff, or don't you remember?"

"As far as I recall," Jeff said, "you never left the platform."

"Oh, but I left again. It was just after you upset the punch bowl out in the corridor— Did I ever tell you about that, Jane dear? Jeff upset the biggest of the punch bowls all over me, and himself, and the Governor. The thing smashed, and the corridor was practically afloat. Anyway, Lieutenant, my shoes and stockings were drenched, and I thought I'd run home and change them at the house, and incidentally see if Henry had made a mistake, and gone there. That's all there was to that."

"And you went to the point, didn't you? Someone saw your car headed that way."

"Oh, no. I never *got* there. When I reached the main road, I thought I saw Henry in the Porter, so I turned right around. But it was just another silvery looking car. And it was so late then that I went on back into the school. I hated to sit there on the platform, all drenched and sticky and dripping, but Jeff made a joke about it when he spoke. The Governor did, too. They were both as drenched and sticky as I was. So you see, Lieutenant, I never went anywhere near the point, or the loft, either."

"Got proof?"

"Oh, dear me, yes," Kate said tranquilly. "Just ask anyone at the school if I wasn't wet and sticky all evening. I never got a chance to change till I got back home with Jeff, later. It's one of the reasons I hurried right home after the Governor left. I hate wet feet."

"You can't put me off with a lot of talk about wet feet!" Hanson said. "You got to have more proof than your feet being wet. You got to prove to me you didn't go to that loft!"

"Don't you think, Hanson," Asey said, "that maybe you jumped to conclusions sort of quick?"

"I do not! I was on the track of all this, even before Lennox called me, Asey. I went down to the sail loft this afternoon, see, and Bert Craddock told me about that cactus in the lavender boot he found. That started me on the track of her."

"The cactus did?" Asey asked. "How, Hanson?"

"Why, it's easy," Hanson said. "Mrs. Lennox has a cactus garden, see? I noticed it, beyond that herb garden. Lennox said it was his wife's. He told me so just now. So, the Dine girl was bringing Mrs. Lennox the cactus for her garden, and she expected to meet Mrs. Lennox there. And—"

"If anyone owns that cactus garden," Jane interrupted suddenly, "I do! Hear that, Smartypants? I do. And if you want to know, *I* killed Irma! Hear that? I killed Irma Dine. *I* killed Henry Slocum!"

Ty Bricker started to speak almost before Jane stopped, and Asey had a feeling that he was picking up a cue.

"You never did!" he said. "*I* killed her! *I* killed him! Don't try to shield me, Jane! I killed them both!"

"You did not! I did!" Jane said.

"Shall I," Jeff said, "take my turn, and say that I killed her, and confuse the estimable Hanson entirely? All right, I did. Now, Hanson, which one of us do you want to go along with you?"

Hanson looked from one to the other, and then he turned to Asey.

"What—what's the matter with 'em?" he asked. "They're all lying!"

"I think," Asey said, "this is a fair sample of what I thought would happen to anyone who was unwise enough to accuse any of this family. If you arrest one of 'em, Hanson, you'll have to arrest 'em all, and Lord have mercy on you when Charles Lennox gets through with you! So long!"

He left so quickly that, although Syl started to run down the hill after him, Asey was in the Porter and speeding along the Shore Road before Syl got anywhere near the puddle by the culvert.

It was eleven o'clock that night when Asey returned to the Slocum house, but he came by an old lane in the rear, and he left his car hidden in a thicket two hills away.

Dr. Cummings was with him, so was Syl, and a considerably chastened Hanson. Asey hadn't heard what Charles Lennox said, but he gathered from Syl's report that Hanson would have preferred a horsewhip to Charles's tongue lashing.

"Take the front," Asey said to him. "Syl, you take that side, an' the doc an' I'll linger over here."

"I still think you're crazy!" Hanson said.

"It can't be any crazier," Dr. Cummings retorted, "than what *you've* thought up so far!"

"Well, anyway," Asey said, "we'll take the chance. You sure you told everyone, doc?"

"Told everyone? I've done everything but sing it through the streets that you've gone rushing off to Boston, that Hanson's gone rushing off to Boston, that neither of you'll be back till tomorrow afternoon, and that you've arrested Irma Dine's brother, and he's in irons— By the way, where is he?"

"I took him up to Barnstable," Hanson said, "just to be on the safe side, in case anyone investigated. Asey, this just doesn't seem possible!"

"Stop maundering, man!" Cummings said, "and go watch the front of the house!"

After Hanson had slipped away in the darkness, the doctor turned to Asey.

"I'd die before I admitted it, in front of him, but it *doesn't* seem possible, Asey! Are you sure?"

Asey nodded.

"I'd gone back to the boat theory this afternoon, after I got Carl Dine's part settled. You see, doc, Jane an' I were there at the sail loft. Jane fell over the body, an' it was there. But it wasn't there when she an' I come back. Now, if the body'd been taken away by car, we'd have seen some trace of a car, or heard some sound of it. We was on one lane, an' we could have heard or seen anythin' on the other. But the only car we heard turned out to be Dine's. It wasn't likely anyone'd tote the body off on their shoulders. So a boat was the solution. I thought so right off the bat, but before we got to know the whole of the story, it seemed too hard, an' too complicated."

"How'd you catch on to Dan Craddock?" Cummings wanted to know.

"Jane brought him up. I only asked her about that signalin' with the flag business to see if I'd get a truthful answer out of her. I still wasn't altogether sure that she an' Ty had told me everythin'. An' the minute she said that old Craddock paddled around the inlet all the time, day in an' day out, I started to prick up my ears. Then all I wanted to know was if he had red hair. An' he did."

"Now how, for God's sakes, did you ever figure that out?"

"Easy, doc. If you're aimin' to commit a murder, an' you figger to go by boat, you still got to take the chance of bein' seen by someone. So you figger you might as well make yourself up to look like someone that people are used to seein' in a boat in that place. Old Craddock's around all the time. Old Craddock's got red hair. So, when you set out to commit your murder, you wear a red wig. N'en if you happen to be seen, people just think it's crazy old Craddock, scavengin' around after his flotsam an' jetsam. My," Asey said, "was I ever glad to get that red wig settled! I yearned to ask about it, but I didn't dare take the chance of lettin' it be known that I'd caught on. I couldn't leave this house quick enough to see if Craddock had red hair! I went there, first off!"

"That sort of figuring," Cummings said, "simply leaves me speechless. If I found a red wig, I should simply be inclined to think that someone was being a comic Irishman in a play. That's as far as I could get. And you even found the boat?"

"Uh-huh. In a little boathouse beyond the school. It's one of them light canvas craft you use for duck huntin'. Y'see, it's three miles from the school to Cod Point an' the sail loft if you go by land, around the Bay. But across it in that canvas boat wouldn't take five minutes. I know. I tried it tonight. He crossed over an' killed the girl, an' then Nosey intervened. Nosey fell all over him, an' in the scuffle, the red wig come off. That was what Jane heard, his tryin' to get the red wig back from Nosey. When she come, he hid in that corner tool room. The minute she left, he picked up the body, put it in the boat, an' departed."

"Not knowing that the flask was left behind," Cummings said, "or that the cactus was there in the lobster pot. Funny what a part a little thing like that cactus plays, isn't it?"

"Yup, it's one of them things," Asey said, "that

you can't take into account beforehand. Like Nosey. You can figger timin', you can figger alibis, but it's out of reason to figger on gettin' tripped up by a cactus plant in a lavender boot in a lobster pot, an' a sort of spaniel with a lot of rugged individualism. He just had to let the wig go. Wasn't nothin' he could do about it. So he took the body, put it in the boat, an' crossed the inlet. Then he pulled the boat, body an' all, into that boathouse. It used to be his land, I found out, till he give it to the school for a playin' field. His land runs up to the bounds."

"And then he went back to that school, and gave his speech?"

"He went right back," Asey said, "an' give his speech. What Jane an' Ty done to Slocum just played into his hands. There was the punch part, first. He found he'd got his feet wet, so he spilled a big bowl of punch all over Mrs. Lennox an' the Governor. That give him a nice reason for havin' wet feet. Remember, the man's practically an actor, doc. He's been in politics seventeen years! See how quick an' easy he twisted Hanson about that dummy business. Hanson was sore one minute, an' eatin' out of his hand the next. See how he grabbed me later Thursday night, an' told me all about Henry Slocum, quick. He got his story in first, see? He done it so good that it wasn't till today I begun to think that maybe Slocum wasn't such an awful villain an' crook."

"When did he take the girl's body from the boat-house?"

"Later on Thursday. That's one of them things I can only guess at, now," Asey said. "But I think you'll find out that after he left the Lennoxes' Thursday night, he went home an' pretended to go to bed. N'en he got up an' walked here to Slocum's, an' killed him, put his body into Slocum's car— Ty'd brought back the key, remember—an' drove it as far's the school. N'en I think he picked up the girl's body an' drove 'em both to the Lennoxes' ice house."

"But I didn't even think he drove!" Cummings said. "I've never seen him drive. He's always being driven by his chauffeur, or someone—"

"He had one of the first Porters ever built," Asey said. "He can drive! Just because he don't, doc, it don't mean he can't!"

"But the chances he took, driving that car of Slocum's! And how'd he get home from the ice house?"

"Not very many chances, doc. What's more deserted than this place up here? What's more deserted than a school at night? What's more deserted than an ice house at night? An' mind that those of us who knew Slocum'd really disappeared had all seen him. We'd given up hunting him. An' the rest of the folks believed he was with that sick friend."

"There were Slocum's friends!" Cummings said.

"Yup. But he knew they'd gone on their merry way to the Gypsy Tea Room an' Bar. I don't know how he got back from the ice house, doc, I'm sure. But he could have walked it, or taken one of the Lennoxes' boats. If it was low tide, he could almost have walked across the inlet. But the cleverest part, doc, was his sendin' the body to you. That got us off the track, an' back to thinkin' about Slocum."

"But the timing of it!" Cummings said. "How could he have dared?"

"He came down from Boston with the Governor," Asey said, "an' anyone who comes down from Boston with the Governor, an' keeps on pointin' it out, is pretty much above suspicion. I found out more, though, tonight. They got to the school at seven. He excused himself to see the janitor about spotlights. That was a few minutes after seven. He was back, tippin' over punch bowls, at seven-thirty, an' no one noticed his leavin' any more than they noticed Mrs. Lennox leavin'. He didn't have to explain anythin'. If anyone pinned him down, why he could find hundreds of people who'd say sure, they saw him between seven an' seven-thirty, they shook his hand. An' they probably did shake his hand some time Thursday night. The timin' fits in like a book with Jane's bumpin' into me, an' what she told me happened before."

Cummings shook his head. "Well, I suppose no one can say he didn't have a motive. It hits you in the face. But there must have been more than his not liking Slocum, and not wanting to get beaten, Asey."

Asey listened for a moment before he answered.

"Thought I heard somethin'," he said, "but it was just Syl. I can see him. We better talk lower. Yup, he had more motive. We're standin' on some of it."

"Slocum's land?"

"The Esty land," Asey said. "Squire Esty owned most of Quashnet, doc, an' his daughter married one of the rich Freemans. Syl told me tonight that the last of the Estys was all but paupers. That didn't sound right. Not if Cod Point was part of their land, an' the golf club. I looked into what I could of that tonight— I found lots of old town books over in the safe at Slocum's store. They owned mints of land, doc. They ought to have died rich an' prosperous."

"What happened?"

"Far as I can figure out, doc, boundaries got miscast. An' at least the Lennoxes' land was sold 'em by Jeff Gage. Now, Slocum got this property for lookin' after the last of the Esty family, an' my guess is, he found out that Jeff had been up to dirty work in the matter of the Estys. I think he looked farther—I didn't have no chance to—an' I think he found out more. That's why Irma Dine went to Boston, don't you see, to look into more things for Slocum!"

"For Slocum?"

"Sure," Asey said. "She an' Slocum couldn't let the Lennoxes know what she was really doin', so she made up this vacation yarn, an' all, like she told Mrs. Hallet. That's why she was troubled, an' said she was in a predicament, an' cried, an' was worried. The more she found out, the worse it got. Now she liked the Lennoxes. They was good to her. But the more she found out about Jeff, the worse it was goin' to be for the Lennoxes. S'pose Jeff got that Cod Point land in a crooked mix-up, miscast bounds, a crooked surveyor, an' some shyster lawyer. An' Jeff sold the land to the Lennoxes. Everythin' seemed all right to them, but s'pose it comes out, now, that Jeff didn't own the land legal? S'pose it comes out that the golf club he controls ain't really his? Or that his Inn ain't his? See?"

"And you think Slocum got on the trail of this through the Esty land?"

"I think so, through that an' his selectman's job. Probably the more things he found, the more it led to, an' I think the harder it was to get actual proof. So the girl went to Boston— Carl said she come back to that boarding house around nine-thirty, an' I wondered then if she hadn't been workin' in some library. Slocum had so much to do, he couldn't leave, see, but she could go an' get real proof that he needed. She was most likely better at that sort of thing than he was. An' she brought everythin' back with her, all her proof—"

"There!" Cummings said. "Stop there. There's a part I don't get at all. How did Jeff know Slocum was on to him?"

"I'd say that Slocum probably was unwise enough to give him some hint," Asey said. "It'd be awful hard to keep things like that to yourself, with Jeff goadin' you, an' makin' you look silly on one platform after another. Slocum was probably tryin' hard to get his proof together to take one good crack at Jeff before elections. One grand disclosin', like. But he must have given somethin' away."

"How'd Jeff know the girl was in Boston?"

"Most likely," Asey said, "he saw her. In some state library, or registry of deeds, or some place at the State House. N'en he followed her, or had some henchman follow her, an' then he sat down, an' decided things had gone far enough, if she was up in Boston lookin' into 'em. So he thought out his plan. All he needed was a red wig an' a blackjack, an' it probably wasn't hard for him to lay hands on either. Then, on Thursday, he called her—"

"You mean, telephoned her?"

"I do. This is a part that stuck me, doc, but I sat down with Carl Dine, an' took a pencil an' paper, an' battled it out with him from what little odds an' ends he heard. The call came from Boston. It wasn't a toll call. The person who told her she had a call didn't say, 'Quashnet is callin',' or anything like that. Just said 'Phone.' Now, Carl remembered enough so I figure that Jeff called her himself, said he was a friend of Slocum's, an' had a message for her that Slocum had been tryin' to get to her, an' couldn't. Carl remembers she said 'Friend?' in a questionin' voice, an' from there on, it was easy. He just had to say that Slocum wanted her to go to the sail loft right away, without bein' seen, bringin' all the papers she had, an' wait for him. Wasn't that neat?"

"Diabolical!" Cummings said. "She wouldn't be inclined to question it. She'd know that Slocum was busy that day, and couldn't keep calling on the chance of finding her in, she'd know that something might have broken, and he wanted what she'd dug out to use in his speech at the school, she wouldn't question the secrecy part of it— It was *all* secret. She'd just go there, and wait!"

"An' when he come, she'd be expectin' Slocum," Asey said. "An' she'd keep on waitin'. If he couldn't have left the school when he first come, she'd still be waitin'. He only had to say he wanted to wash his hands, or somethin', an' slip out."

"What's all that," Cummings said, "about goodly villains with smiling cheeks, and nice looking red apples with worms? And do you really think he'll be fooled, and turn up here?"

"Don't forget, he hasn't had a chance to come here an' look through that little tin safe with the red roses that Slocum has in that dinin' room," Asey said. "He's got to go through that, to make sure there's nothin' incriminatin' lyin' around. He didn't dare take the chance of lookin' on Thursday, with two bodies to get out of the way. An' Syl was here, an' Hanson's men, an' Slocum's friends. He hasn't had a chance at that. An' his eyes kept strayin' to it this evenin', doc. He could hardly keep his eyes off it. An' I told you, when he burned up them notes of Jane's an' Kate Lennox's, I think he burned up somethin' else. Some sort of legal paper. I saw a couple pieces of that blue paper they bind 'em with, an' I saw him lookin' at 'em two or three times. He may not come tonight, doc, but I think he will, if you spoke your piece about me an' Hanson bein' away. Sooner or later, he'll come."

Jeff Gage came, at three o'clock that morning. He came on foot, and once inside Slocum's house he went straight for the little tin safe with the red roses in the corner of the dining room. The four outside watched as he trained his square, lantern-like flash on the lock, and went to work opening it.

They waited till he had it open, and the contents of the safe spread around him, and then Asey touched Hanson's arm.

"Now!" he said.

Jeff shot once wildly at Hanson, before Asey and Syl grabbed him. And, a second later, the doctor wrenched from his hand the pair of scissors he had picked up in the scuffle.

"No vein cutting!" Cummings said. "We're taking you whole!"

Jeff's answering tirade was something that Asey hoped he would not remember, along with the expression on Jeff's face.

"Loathsome!" Cummings said as Asey left him at his doorstep later. "Utterly loathsome! He hanged himself in the first sentence. What a horrible old man!"

"He was gettin' back his composure, though,"

Asey said, "before we dropped him an' Hanson off at the jail. He may try to wiggle out."

"All his friends, and all his composure and all his money can't help him after what we saw, and heard him say," Cummings said. "Asey, why did you leave Syl at your house first?"

"He looked tired," Asey said. "Needs sleep."

"Where are you going? Are you going to try out that infernal car?"

"I am," Asey told him. "I been yearnin' to since Thursday. An' at this time of the mornin', an' with all the chores done, I think it's perfectly safe. Doc, there's a package on your doorstep."

"What? My God, where? Where, Asey? I don't see it!"

"It's there."

It should be, Asey knew. Syl had promised faithfully that it would be.

He waited till Cummings tore off the wrappings, and listened to Cummings's startled exclamation as he felt the contents.

"Asey, it's a fish! A dead fish!"

Asey chuckled as he pressed the starter button.

"What are you laughing about?" Cummings demanded.

"Don't you get it, doc? Another Criminal Cod!"